"We both know you're not a domestic, don't we now?"

Katie was livid. "And you think that gives you the right to force yourself on me?"

"Come on, love," Harry taunted. "Don't tell me you didn't enjoy kissing me, because I know you did. I would think that my aunt would have picked out a more experienced candidate, though."

"I haven't the slightest idea what you're talking about!"

A wide grin spread across his face. "I wouldn't put it past Aunt Grace and my sister to work up some double-barreled scheme. Anybody who would choose this route as a shortcut to Ohio needs her brain transplanted. Don't be alarmed, though. I always manage to uncover the plot before the trap is sprung."

The only trap, as far as Katie was concerned, was the one fate had caught her in by leading her to Harry King's door!

EMMA GOLDRICK describes herself as a grandmother first and an author second. She was born and raised in Puerto Rico where she met her husband, a career military man from Massachusetts. His postings took them all over the world, which often led to peculiarities—such as the Christmas they arrived in Germany before their furniture, or the fact that their daughter learned Japanese before English. Emma uses the places she's been as backgrounds for her books, but just in case she runs short of settings, this prolific author and her husband are always making new travel plans.

Books by Emma Goldrick

These books may be available at your local bookseller.

Don't miss any of our special offers. Write to us at the following address for information on our newest releases.

Harlequin Reader Service
901 Fuhrmann Blvd., P.O. Box 1397, Buffalo, NY 14240
Canadian address: P.O. Box 2800, Postal Station A,
5170 Yonge St., Willowdale, Ont. M2N 6J3

EMMA GOLDRICK

the over-mountain man

Harlequin Books

TORONTO • NEW YORK • LONDON
AMSTERDAM • PARIS • SYDNEY • HAMBURG
STOCKHOLM • ATHENS • TOKYO • MILAN

To Polly King,
who taught us to love mountains

Harlequin Presents first edition June 1986
ISBN 0-373-10890-7

Original hardcover edition published in 1985
by Mills & Boon Limited

CHAPTER ONE

IT was five o'clock in the morning when the layby appeared on the right-hand side of the twisting mountain road. With a sigh of relief she turned the wheel, drove the little red Volkswagen out on to the rough grass and turned off the motor. There was an old wooden signpost about six feet away. She unfolded her five feet ten inches from the tiny box of a car, stretched mightily, and wandered over to the sign. A full moon graced the horizon to the west of her, and in its brilliant light she read 'Spivey Gap, Great Smokey Mountains. Elevation 3252.'

She rubbed the back of her neck to relieve the tensions from the long drive, and ruffled her fingers through the tight bronze cap of curls that lay in confusion against her head. Spivey Gap? What in heaven's name ever led me to take this 'short cut'? Somebody said something—I wish I could remember! A short cut from Charlotte, North Carolina, to Humbersville, Ohio. Who said it? Great day! Eubie Fairfield said it! The clown who finally convinced me to head for Ohio and home—seven weeks early for sister Marion's wedding. How about that? I'm lost in the mountains between Carolina and Tennessee, and all on the word of the biggest idiot who ever played baseball!

She was laughing quietly to herself as she sauntered back to the car. It was chillier than she had expected for an early morning in late August. There was no sign of a breeze. She opened the car door and fumbled in the back seat for her cardigan. Her camera cases, the tools of her trade, filled the seat. She up-ended one of the Minolta cases, found a sweater, and slipped it on, a wry grin on her mobile tanned face. She ran both hands through her hair again, and leaned against the top of the car.

Eubie Fairfield, probably the worst outfielder in the Carolina League. 'Big bat, big mouth, little glove,' the sports editor of the paper had written. 'Every fly ball hit to left field is an adventure when Eubie is there!' She had been dating him for two months, and had already concluded he had little to offer except his height. And then, just before he boarded the bus on the last road trip of the season with the team, he had called her.

'I'll be back in fifteen days, babe,' he had said. 'And when I do we're going to do something about your brash little maiden act.'

'You can't cure brashness overnight,' she had laughed.

'No,' he returned, 'but we can cure maidenhood!'

What with all her other troubles—homesickness, Marion's wedding, the problem of working in the field of sports photography, essentially a man's world, and now Eubie's little promise—all that had been just enough for her to resign from World Wide Photos, pack her few things in a bag, and head for Ohio. Which, in turn, had put her, early in the morning, near the crest of the Great Smokey Mountains, the section of the Appalachian Range which divided the Atlantic plain of the United States from the great internal valleys of the Ohio, Mississippi, and Tennessee Rivers. She shivered again as she looked out into the silvery moonlight, now beginning to pale under the threat of pre-dawn in the east.

She stretched one more time, then crammed herself back inside the car. She shifted into gear, drove over the crest of the pass, and nearly swallowed her tongue. The road ahead of her went straight downhill for about fifty yards, and then disappeared into a thick white layer of fog. Fog that hung over everything in the valley, obliterating all signs of life, as if a painter had wiped the canvas clean. It was as if she were in an aeroplane, skipping over the top bank of clouds. Route 19W seemed to have poised itself on top of the mountain, and dived off into nothing.

The brakes squealed as she jammed then on, and the little red light on the dashboard blinked at her a dozen times or more before it quivered out. Well, she told herself, you can hardly turn back. As best as she could remember there was nothing behind her but mountain roads, dark forbidding mountain roads, until you came to the village of Bald Creek. Which had been shrouded in darkness when she had driven through some two hours before. And the little red light on the dashboard wasn't blinking any more. It glared at her in righteous wrath, saying something important in a language Katie could not fathom. Anything mechanical was anathema to her—except for her cameras, over which she had laboured with love since she was fifteen.

'Oh murder!' she snarled in exasperation, pounding on the steering wheel to relieve her frustrations. But there seemed to be no alternative. Turning back was out of the question. Stopping by the side of the road to out-wait the fog was equally distasteful. With a muttered prayer she took her foot off the brake, shifted into second gear, and urged the little car forward into the fog. It swallowed her, car and all.

She could barely see six feet in front of her. Her foot automatically switched the lights to low-beam as her hands moved the car over to the crown of the road. She aimed her tiny hood ornament down the white line that marked the highway's centre, and leaned forward over the steering wheel, taking full advantage of her height to get her nose close to the windscreen. Her grip on the wheel tightened, and the car slowed to five miles an hour. The road bucked and twisted under the wheels, and her eyes, straining forward into the fog, began to water from over-concentration. The red light on the dashboard came on again and glared balefully at her.

For twenty minutes she felt her way downward, deep into the fog, trying to wish herself clear. The little engine behind her pushed valiantly, but it had lost its smooth chatter, and was beginning to make fearful noises. That is, it did until it gave one dismal clank and stopped altogether. The glaring red light went out.

She pulled up the handbrake, shifted to neutral, and hit the starter button. Nothing happened. Absolutely nothing. She leaned back in her seat and pounded both fists on the steering wheel. 'Why me?' she yelled out at the fog. There was no answer. She rolled down her window and watched warily as tiny tendrils of fog weaved into the car, bringing a wet chill, and a fearful warning. 'You are all alone. The world has disappeared,' voices whispered in her ear.

She leaned out the window. 'Now what do I do?' she roared into the mist. There was a soft sigh of wind in unseen trees. She sniffed appreciatively at the sweet pine scent in the air. If the wind blew, the fog was bound to be blown away, wasn't it? Or was it? In the Ohio flatlands fog was an occasional thing that clung to the rivers. Here, where hundreds of little streams and creeks ran into the Tennessee, behind the thousand-and-one dams of the Tennessee Valley Authority, there would always be moisture in the air. 'But it can't get any worse,' she assured herself, dragging up every cliché she had ever heard. 'And it's bound to be all downhill from here.'

As she heard her own voice she slapped her forehead in disgust. Of course! She had passed over the crest of the mountain, and it *was* all downhill from here. She was still laughing at herself as she made sure that the gearshift was in neutral, and then released the hand brake. The little car began to roll, gently at first, and then much faster. She shifted her foot to the brake pedal, curbing the car's tendency to build up to forty miles an hour, and hunched forward in her seat again.

She saw the glow of the lights as she came around a deep bend, just in time to slam on her brakes. The glow gradually decentralised itself as she allowed the car to

slide down towards it. Two bright lights, each surrounded by a halo, gleaming at her from the right-hand
side of the road.

Cautiously she turned the car loose. It glided forward
until she could see a large paved area beside the road, an
area that looked dimly like a parking lot. Two cars were
already at rest there.

'Well, at least it's *someplace*,' she sighed as she
steered her battered car into a space beside a shining
black Mercedes. When she crawled out of the car to
stretch she noticed that the second car was a more
commonplace four-door Reliant. 'So it's not so bad,
Hilda,' she told her trusty little VW. She patted her car
affectionately on its roof, and started to walk towards
the lights.

There were two stone pillars, about ten feet high, at
the back end of the parking lot, and on top of each was
an electric globe. She walked through the gateway
formed by the pillars. Immediately she felt the hollow-
ness of wood beneath her feet. She stopped and bent
over to investigate. She was on a bridge, some twelve
feet wide, leading into the fog towards another light, two
hundred feet or more away.

She fumbled her way to the side of the bridge until her
hand discovered a steel railing, set about waist high.
Going cautiously, she used the rail as a guide. After
twenty feet of bridge she stepped off on to a white-
pebbled path, and kept going. The light ahead of her was
coming through a fan of glass set over the top of a heavy
wooden door. Nothing could be seen of the house which
contained it. She fumbled her way up three steps,
crossed a wooden veranda, and stopped in front of the
door.

A huge brass door knocker in the shape of a lion's
head glared at her from the exact middle of the door.
Too weary now to puzzle it all out, she grabbed the lion's
head and beat a rapid tattoo on the door. That is, she
banged the knocker three times, and was about to give it

another when knocker, door, and all were snatched away from her, and she was looking down a large well-lit hall, half-blocked by a blurred male form. All she could tell of him was that he was taller by inches than she was, and for some reason that fact made her feel just the slightest bit welcome.

'Well, come in, come in!' His voice was a deep *basso profundo*. Which immediately shook Katie's confidence. Among other things she was an opera buff, and she knew not only that the tenor was always the hero, but the *basso profundo* was most always the darkest of villains!

'Don't stand in the damned door!' The voice was exasperated. She wished she could make out more of the man who went with it. He grabbed at one of her wrists and pulled her into the hall. 'I've been waiting since six o'clock last night,' he told her, urging her down the hall. 'We expected you at least by midnight!'

'Well, I left at nine last night, and drove as fast as I could,' she said defensively. 'Expecting me? I—'

'Of course we were expecting you.' He had urged her to the depth of the hall, behind a set of beautiful mahogany stairs that curved gently up to the floor above. 'I called the agency six times. They promised us faithfully that you'd be here!'

'And here I am,' she gasped, wondering what in the world was going on. 'But where is—'

'No time for explanations!' He opened the door under the stairs. 'Do something about that.'

'That' was a little boy, about eighteen months old, sitting in the middle of a hastily rigged nursery, crying his heart out.

'Do something?' she stammered.

'Come off it,' he roared. 'I know you're not a nurse, but the agency said you would be willing to try. Any woman ought to be able to make a kid stop crying! He's been bellowing since noontime yesterday!'

'Any woman?' she asked feebly.

'Well, almost any woman.' He modified his statement slightly, with a tone of disgust.

'He means me, honey.' The voice came from behind her. Katie turned around to the door. It was half-occupied by a beautiful little blonde woman, leaning against the jamb. She was dressed in a flowery blue translucent nightgown, covered slightly by a transparent yellow négligé, and leaving somewhat more of her showing than the movies usually permit. Which was the thought running through Katie's head. I've fallen into a crazy movie set, she told herself. There's the kid, she's the beautiful heroine, and he's the villain. And where does that leave me?

'All right, Eloise,' he said. 'You had your chance, and you blew it.'

'I'm an actress, darling, not a baby-sitter. If I had known what was going to happen I never would have come. Some week in the country this is!'

'And how was I to know that my sister would roar through here in a fit of frenzy and drop her brat on me, while she ran after that fancy-dan husband of hers! Well, the kid's still crying, Miss—?'

'Russel,' Katie answered. 'Katherine Russel.'

'. . . so do something. Quick!'

'Quickly,' Katie muttered under her breath, but she could not help but jump as if he had snapped a bullwhip at her. She walked over towards the child. He struggled to his feet, still crying. Katie knelt down and held out her arms. 'Come on, darling,' she chanted softly. The little boy reduced his hoarse uproar to a whimper. She clicked her tongue at him a time or two, and he started to wobble in her direction. She swept him up, cuddling him against her breast, running her hands up and down his soft body. All the time she crooned to him, one of those little tunes she remembered her mother using on her five young nephews and nieces. The boy put his tired head, shrouded in blond curls, down in the shadow of her bronze curls, and stopped the noise. She jiggled him up and down a few times, soothingly. And there you go again, she lectured herself. You've always been a sucker for little boys!

'See! I told you so! Any woman could do it!' the man declared. He seemed to talk in exclamation marks, Katie noted. The idea brought a tiny giggle to her lips. The baby responded with one of his own.

'If you're blunderbussing at me,' Eloise drawled, 'you're wasting your ammunition. I didn't contract out to be a nursemaid. But I *am* happy you've got one. Can she cook? I'd like to get a decent meal in this mausoleum!'

'The child is soaking wet,' Katie interjected. 'He needs a clean set of diapers.'

'I would think you could at least get your own breakfast,' he snorted. 'There's more to life than just looking beautiful.'

'That's not what you said Thursday night upstairs,' Eloise snapped back at him. 'Well, can she?'

'Diapers,' Katie repeated. 'It's very urgent.'

'Diapers? How the hell would I know!' His face had finally come into the light, so Katie could get a good look at him. He was definitely a good head taller than she. His face was triangular, broad at the forehead, coming down to an almost pointed chin. Blue eyes. Brilliant sky-blue, deepset, with a twinkle that belied the harshness of his words. A half-day growth of red beard matched the flame of his unruly hair. He was dressed in a crimson bathrobe, sloppy slippers, and apparently nothing else.

'His mother left a bag?' Katie probed.

'A bag! Of course. Over there by the table.'

Katie left the two of them to their argument, and carried the child over to the side-table. She stretched the boy out and began to strip off his soaking pyjamas. Free of restraint, he kicked and crowed hoarsely. She held him down with a tickling hand on his stomach, while her other hand searched through the crowded tote bag. She was unable to find what she needed with only the one hand. 'Would one of you come over here and help?' she asked desperately.

'Yes. What do I do?' He was at her elbow so fast that she jumped in surprise. 'Play with him,' she instructed. 'Don't let him fall off the table.' And watch out that he doesn't squirt you, she added under her breath.

Her two-hand search quickly turned out diapers, wipes, anti-rash cream, pins, and plastic pants. She brushed him aside, and covered the child with practical ease.

'For not being a nurse, you do that pretty skilfully,' he commented.

'Three nieces, two nephews,' she returned through a mouthful of pins. 'I'm a practising professional aunt. And if you had put some cream on his bottom last night he wouldn't be sore this morning, and that's why he was bellowing. Unless he's starving. When did you last feed him?'

'Last night at supper time.'

'What?'

'What did I feed him? Well, we all had hamburgers, and he—I really don't remember.'

'Charming,' she snapped. 'Very nutritional. You'd better show me where the kitchen is.'

'Oh, you do cook! How lovely,' Eloise chimed in.

'Only for babies,' Katie snarled, beginning to feel a little put-upon. 'Babies, and little old ladies over sixty.'

'That's great,' he said as he guided her back down the corridor to the kitchen. 'My Aunt Grace is my housekeeper, but she's laid up with a bad attack of arthritis. It's the weather, you know. She qualifies.'

'Qualifies for what?' Katie asked, as her hands sorted through the refrigerator, her busy mind only half-listening to what he had to say. Another loony? Does his aunt qualify as an inmate, or is she sensibly hiding from this pair?

'For your cooking,' he said. 'She's sixty-two and likes

scrambled eggs. Eggs and bacon. I don't mind that myself. You don't think . . . ?'

'No. That's my trouble,' Katie snapped in an exasperated tone. 'I don't think often enough. Everybody tells me that. Now suppose you tell me who the devil you are, and then you can tell me why little Miss Eloise here can't scramble an egg. Or maybe you could manage to burn a piece of toast all by yourself? Here, hold the baby.' She thrust the child at him. He barely managed to catch the boy under the armpits. The child immediately began to cry. With an apologetic half-smile he gave the boy back to her.

'My name is King. Harry King.' He paused for effect, looking at her as if she should have recognised the name. When she gave no sign he continued, 'The boy's name is Jon. My sister Amanda is his mother. She's gone to Charlotte for a few days. Aunt Grace is my housekeeper. Ordinarily everything would be running fine, but Aunt Grace is upstairs in bed. She had a sudden attack two days ago, just minutes after Eloise arrived. And of course Eloise is my . . . er . . . houseguest. You may have seen her on television. Eloise Norris?'

'For heaven's sakes, you don't have to go around explaining me to the kitchen help,' Eloise drawled. 'Just let her get on with the cooking!'

'Then maybe you'll hold the baby?' Katie asked sarcastically.

'Me? Not on your life. Put him on the floor. Or back in his room. Or something!'

Which seemed to be the way of things with both of them, Katie thought. Exclamation mark conversations. Snappy repartee. And not a minute's worth of help. No wonder his aunt took to her bed. She moved the child from her shoulder to her hip. There was something charming about the little fellow's face. Charming—and familiar? It had to do with the lightness of his curls, the blue of his eyes, and the long curled eyelashes—all wasted on a boy! But first things first, she told herself.

Lord, how tired I am. Get the child fed and out of the way of this hapless pair, and then see about Aunt Grace, wherever she may be hiding. And then my car! Oh Lord, don't forget my car!

She searched the shelves and storage compartments of the large old-fashioned kitchen, but could find nothing in the way of baby food. So something soft. Scrambled eggs for him, too? I wonder how many teeth he's got? She slipped her finger into the baby's mouth, and he promptly demonstrated that he was well equipped.

Katie managed to rescue the finger, shaking it in the air to relieve the pressure of those sharp little fangs. It took a bit of doing to hold back the tears. She walked over to the sink and stuck her finger under the cold water spout.

'Bit you, did he?' King enquired. He made it sound as if it were a common occurrence.

'No. Of course not,' she muttered. 'Do you happen to have a highchair, or something?'

'Highchair? Oh, for the boy. No. I'll improvise something.'

'And I'll be in the living room,' Eloise chimed in.

'And I'm glad to see the backs of both of you,' Katie muttered to herself. Riding the baby on her ample hip, she pillaged the refrigerator of eggs, cheese, milk, and butter. It was a difficult juggling act to break six eggs into a bowl without it all landing on the floor, but every time she started to set Jon down he howled. The boy was all eyes as he watched. One of her curls swung within his range as she bent over. His pudgy little hands seized on it and gave it a yank that brought tears to her eyes. She rummaged beneath the work surface until she found a steel mixing bowl and a large wooden spoon. She knelt down, sitting the baby at her feet, close to the table.

Two demonstration whacks with the spoon on the rim of the bowl produced a clang that grabbed the child's interest. She watched for a moment while he demonstrated his enthusiasm, then stood up, massaging her right arm.

'Heavy, is he?' She glared at King as he came back into the room. 'No highchairs,' he announced, 'but how about this?' *This* was an infant's car seat, cleverly attached to a tall bar stool. It was high enough for adult comfort, and the straps looked heavy enough to hold the most active child.

'That's marvellous,' Katie marvelled. 'Very clever. I suppose you read about it somewhere or other?'

'Read about it?' he asked indignantly. 'I don't copy other people's ideas. I'm an inventor.'

'You mean you make your living inventing things?'

'Exactly. That's a fine tan you've got, Katherine. Have you been in the Caribbean on vacation?'

'Hmm? You mean me?' She was pouring the beaten egg mixture into the hot pan, and did not want to make a mistake about it. 'I've been in Charlotte—oh, I see what you mean. Yes, it's a tan, but I get it from sunlamps. I don't have a lot of time for sunbathing. It gives a more uniform tan, you know. I look that way all over.'

'Well!' There were devil-glints in those blue eyes. 'I'll have to see that to believe it!'

Oh brother, Katie sighed to herself. One of those kind. Me and my big mouth. 'You'll just have to take my word for it,' she assured him primly. 'I don't give shows or sell tickets.'

'Too bad,' he replied as he watched her hands gently stir the eggs in the pan. He was definitely laughing at her. She clenched her one free hand. As always, her first reaction was to hit out. And her second, too, for that matter. Instead, she began the cumbersome task of separating bacon strips from the package she had found in the back corner of the meat compartment.

When the bacon was done to her own taste, crisp and brown, finger-eatable, she sopped up some of the fat with a paper towel, and reheated the eggs in the same pan. In minutes the breakfast was ready.

She snatched up the little boy, strapped him into his improvised seat, and brought him a plastic bowl of eggs and a tiny plastic glass of milk. 'Now you get to work,' she told Harry. 'At this age they like to try to feed themselves. You just have to see that more gets in his mouth than on the floor. And watch the milk. Kids are not too good at finding their mouth with a glass.'

'Right, General,' he replied.

Why, he's still laughing at me, Katie told herself. Where have I ever met such a disgusting, arrogant man before?

'And where will you be while I'm doing all this risky work?'

She had found a larger plate, stocked it with eggs, bacon, and toast, and loaded it on a tray. 'You said your aunt was bedridden. I'm going to take her a breakfast tray. Only I can't find the coffee pot.'

'Oh that,' he chuckled, but his face had turned an embarrassed red. 'I used it for an experiment that blew up—and I've not had time to buy a new one. We're using instant. You go ahead. I'll fix a couple of cups and bring them up. It's the first room to the right at the head of the stairs.'

Katie balanced the tray on one hand and started out into the hall.

'Ah, breakfast,' Eloise said from the living room chair where she was scanning a copy of *Cosmopolitan* magazine. 'Just set it right there on the end table.'

'This is for the invalid,' Katie snapped, and stalked up the stairs. What in the world am I doing, she asked herself as her feet stumbled on the heavily carpeted stairs. All I have to do is to tell them it's a big mistake. And then I can find a telephone to get my car repaired, and *voilà*, out of this madhouse I go. Why don't I?

At the head of the stairs she stopped long enough to look out of the window at the end of the corridor. The massive fog bank was still with them, covering everything.

'Well, that's *one* reason why I don't,' she muttered. But there was another reason niggling at her mind. It had to do with—the baby? Or its uncle? It's almost like coming into a theatre in the middle of the movie. You hate to leave until you see how it all comes out! She brushed that idea away. She knew she was a sensible, pragmatic woman—even though all her friends called her an incurable romantic!

She knocked at the proper door, and heard a tired voice authorising entry. Katie backed in, pushing the door open with her hip, holding the tray in two hands. When she turned round she found herself in an over-large bedroom, decorated in white and gold, with a huge four-poster bed directly opposite her, between two large windows. A tiny thimbleful of a woman was sitting up in the bed, her back comfortable against two large pillows, with sheets pulled high enough so that a lace collar was all that could be seen of her nightgown. A pair of gold-rimmed glasses were perched on her button nose, and a book lay open in her right hand. She looked at Katie over the tops of her glasses.

'And just who might you be,' the tired voice quavered. Katie winced. If there was anything that being raised in a large family taught, it was respect for one's elders. Not just a respect for their needs, but for the sharp minds they hid behind benign faces.

'I'm Katie Russel, ma'am,' she responded. 'I've brought your breakfast.'

'Well, don't just stand at the door, Katie. Bring it over here. My, you are a very—'

'Large?' Katie offered.

'Yes. The very word. A very large girl, aren't you? Put the tray down right there. You must have cooked it too. Is that woman gone?' There was just a touch of despair in her voice as she spat out the question.

'You mean Eloise?' Katie set the tray down on the bedside table, straightened out the sheets, then balanced the tray across the elderly woman's knees.

'She's downstairs in the living room, waiting for me to make her some breakfast.'

Aunt Grace must have caught the touch of sarcasm in her voice. 'And how long will she have to wait?'

'Until it gets so cold that . . . well, until it gets as cold as that. I hope you like scrambled eggs. Can you hold a spoon? My grandmother has arthritis too, and she has trouble with spoons.'

'You are a dear, well-mannered child,' the older woman said. 'But there's nothing wrong with me.' She demonstrated by picking up the fork and demolishing a large segment of the eggs. 'My, am I hungry.'

'But there's nothing wrong? I thought that Mr King said you were in poor condition. That's why I was worried!'

'He was wrong, Katie. I may call you that, may I? I lied to him. I just could not bring myself to be in this house with that horrible woman here. She means to marry him, you know. What a terrible thing to happen! These eggs are nice. What is the extra little flavour you added?'

'A pinch of grated cheese, ma'am, with just a flavouring from the bacon, and one diced tomato. I hope you like it?'

'I like it exceptionally well. And I must tell you how happy I am to see you here. You appear to be just the type of girl that Harry needs. Sit down here on the bed and tell me about Katie Russel.' The directions were accompanied by a pat on the blankets to indicate where she should sit. Katie complied. 'Now, you will call me Aunt Grace. Tell me all about yourself.'

'I—I don't quite know what to say,' Katie stammered. This lady had all the attitudes and inflections of Grandmother Russel. A most sweet and loving woman, who could get information out of anyone—man, woman, or child—as simply as if she were peeling an artichoke. And before Katie realised, she had displayed her life from her first birthday party until the day before yesterday.

'And so you see,' she ended, 'I got lost in the mountain, and my engine stopped dead before I got to your gate and I knocked on the door and they thought I was the home-help come to take care of the baby, and things have been so rushed that I haven't had a chance yet to tell Harry—Mr King.' At which point in the recital she ran out of breath and came to a full stop.

Aunt Grace raised one eyebrow reflectively. Then she picked up a crisp of bacon and nibbled at it, deep in thought.

'And isn't that nice,' she finally concluded. 'We have no need to tell Harry. We mustn't overburden the poor boy with too much information. How very nice. Stand up and twirl around.'

Never thinking to question, Katie complied, then enquired by a look and got no answer. 'I haven't had a chance to change,' she apologised. 'I left Carolina in the rain, and I put on my oldest jeans and shirt, and I—'

'You're just a shade too thin for your height, my dear. How tall are you?'

'Five foot ten in my stocking feet, ma'am. I haven't been eating too regularly lately, I suppose.'

'Lovely face, my dear. Such smooth skin, so nicely rounded. And I like your hair. Russet natural curls?' She didn't wait for an answer. 'And those lovely green eyes. Harry's exactly six feet four, did you know that? Yes, you'll do very well. Tiny waist, fine rounded hips—'

Katie began to get the feeling that she was standing on the auction block, being checked out as a brood mare. And she wasn't quite sure how to respond.

'But somewhat—lacking, perhaps, above?'

Katie smiled, and looked down to where her tiny breasts were having no difficulty at all concealing themselves from public view. 'Well, it saves a lot of money,' she said wryly. 'I never have to buy bras. What did you mean, I'll do? As soon as I get my car repaired, I'm off to Ohio.'

'Ah. Of course. Of course. But it might take longer

than you think to get your car repaired. And in the meantime, you will have to remain here as—Oh, there you are, Harry. Did you bring coffee for Katie, too?'

'For who?'

'For Katie. I was just telling her that she must consider herself our guest until you can get her car repaired. Don't you think?'

'I'm afraid I don't understand, Aunt Grace. Katherine was hired—' He stopped talking to watch his aunt slowly swing her head from side to side. 'Well, okay. You can explain it to me later. Here's your coffee. And I brought up my own, and I thought I would—'

'Would immediately go back downstairs and bring up another cup for Katie. Do you take cream and sugar, my dear?'

'No—I drink coffee black,' Katie protested. 'And I can go down and get my own. And have some breakfast, too, if I may. Who's with the baby?'

'Eloise is minding the kid. She's not entirely helpless, you know.'

'That's something you will have to prove to me,' his aunt told him in glacial tones. 'Maybe you had better go and have your breakfast, Katherine. Lovely name. My great-grandmother was named Katerine. Did you know that, Harry? A lovely woman. Presented her husband with six children. Where was I? Oh yes, you go ahead, Katie. I'll have a talk with this nephew of mine, and join you later.'

Katie got up and almost ran to the door. Both of them were talking, neither listening, as she closed the door behind her. She stopped at the head of the stairs, one hand on the round pomegranate knob of the newell post. It seemed almost impossible to control her shaking nerves. What have I got myself into, she almost screamed at herself. They're mad! Every one of them!

Well, it's too late to turn back, and too soon to run. She drew herself up to her full height, controlled her breathing, and stilled the vibrations in her legs. Outside the window the fog bank glared at her, as if waiting for the glass to break so that it could get at her. She took more deep breaths, and forced her hands to unclench. There were little red marks in each of her palms, where her nails had almost pierced the skin. She held them up in front of her, giggling almost hysterically.

'Welcome to Never-Never Land, Katie,' she said, and started down the stairs.

CHAPTER TWO

IT was the sound of the baby crying that hurried Katie's steps. She found him in the kitchen all alone, holding on to one of the table legs to keep himself upright. Eloise was gone. So was the entire platter of bacon and eggs. Kate could feel a surge of anger flush through her system. But the baby must come first. She held out her arms and made love-noises. Little Jon glanced at her, turned off his waterfall, and wobbled over for comfort.

'Back to square one,' she sighed as she ran her hand over the little man's bottom. 'Or square one-half, no less!' She bundled him up on her hip again, chuckling as she recalled Aunt Grace's comments, but thankful to have a place to rest the heavy child. And then back to the nursery. As she went by the living room door she could see Eloise daintily picking at the last of the bacon. 'Don't forget to clean up my room,' the actress called after her as she thumped down the corridor.

'Don't forget to clean up my room,' Katie mimicked as she lay the boy down on the table to change his wet diaper. 'Don't forget—oh you poor little darling. You need a bath!'

She pinned the new diaper, grabbed a handful of clean clothes, swung the baby back on her hip, and went hunting for a bathroom. She found one on the second floor, three doors down the hall. It was tiny, but well-decorated. She started the water, and laughed as the baby, realising what was to come, gurgled in glee. There was an assortment of bottles on the glass shelf over the washbasin. She picked up a bottle of bubble bath at hazard and used it liberally in the tub. Jon began to bounce up and down in expectation. She tested the water temperature with her elbow and plunged the baby

25

into the water. Pandemonium broke loose—in a small way.

'You like this?' She laughed at him as the baby began to beat at the tiny bubbles with the flat of his hand. She left him to his own devices, only occasionally getting in a lick with the flannel at strategic places where his antics had failed to splash him clean. She had tucked a towel under her chin and across her breasts, and was just about to lift the child out, when both doors to the bathroom opened almost simultaneously.

'So this is where you've got to,' Harry King announced from the hallway. 'I looked all over the ground floor for you.'

'Just what are you doing with that brat in my bathroom?' Eloise grated from the other doorway. Behind her, Katie could see the outline of a lavishly decorated bedroom, like a rococo harem.

'I—' Katie started to say.

'Get him out of here,' Eloise demanded in a harsh voice. 'How do you expect me to keep myself clean if I have to share a bathroom with that messy child?'

'That's enough, Eloise,' Harry commanded. There was evidently something unusual in his tone that cut Eloise off without another word. Master of his world, Katie thought, as she watched the expression on his face. I'm glad he's not talking to me.

'We were just leaving,' she told them both. She wrapped the towel around the baby, pulled out the plug, and started towards the door.

'Well, aren't you at least going to clean the tub?' Eloise demanded. Katie had had about enough. Her all-night drive, followed by a hectic three hours in this strange house, were proving to be too much for her usually placid temper. She turned around, walked directly over to the other woman, and looked down at her.

'No,' she said softly. 'Get your little pinkies dirty for a change. And the next time I go to all that work, don't grab my breakfast. I did expect to eat something myself, if you must know.'

'Well, I do—Harry? Aren't you going to do something about this—this impertinence?'

'No. At least I don't think I am,' he replied. He was turned so that only Katie could see the sparkle in his brilliant blue eyes. 'No, I don't think I want to say anything to her. I've just found out that she's not the home-help we've been waiting for. She's a professional photographer who got lost on her way home to Ohio.'

'A photographer? My God, Harry, I have to work with them, but I don't have to live with them. Why would you hire a—'

'You're not listening to me,' he interrupted. 'She's got nothing to do with you, and I didn't hire her. She just came. Or so Aunt Grace believes.'

He's enjoying it all, Katie told herself. Look at the gleam in his eyes. He enjoys giving everybody the needle. Even his—his houseguest. 'She's a photographer—or so Aunt Grace believes.' What could he mean by that? He thinks I'm a burglar in disguise? I can see that a few days in this man's company will really drive me over the wall!

'And now, if you'll excuse me,' Katie interjected, 'I'll take the baby back to wherever he's supposed to sleep, and leave you two to wrestle about your bathroom. Here we go, little Jon.'

'I think I'd better go with you,' Harry said. 'You haven't been assigned a room yet, so we'll get one for you now. Down the corridor to the right. I think we'll put you right across the hall from Aunt Grace.' He led the way, opening the door on a small suite of rooms, decorated in a pastel yellow. 'You have a bedroom in here, a sitting room, and a separate bath. You did tell Aunt Grace you would stay for a few days?'

'I guess I did,' she responded glumly. 'It was pretty hard not to. I couldn't seem to get a word in edgewise.' She dumped the baby down on the bed, and began to dry him off. 'And as for that—that lady friend of yours, you'd better tell her that all photographers are not like the ones she seems to know. Some of us eat politely, dress adequately, and hardly ever spit on the sidewalk!'

'Hey—okay,' he laughed. 'I apologise. For both of us. I didn't mean to step on your shadow. Eloise has probably been mixing with the wrong side of the business. I'll speak to her.'

He stared at her for a moment, then, without a word, took her by the shoulders and manoeuvred her directly into the lamplight. 'Why that really is red, isn't it,' he mused. 'Dark, but red all the same. And those crazy curls—are they real too?'

She pushed away from him, and tried to brush his hands off her shoulders, without success. Her slender frame shook with her indignation, until he felt the warning tremors under his palms. Almost regretfully, he released her. 'I was just curious,' he said.

'Well, I'm not for sale,' she snapped at him, 'so I don't care to have you handle the goods. Yes, my hair is real, but not red. It's more like bronze, or russet. Not bright, like yours.' She could hardly keep the awe out of her voice. His hair was brilliantly red, flanked with gold, and set smoothly around his head in a close cropping, a little longer at the nape than one would expect, but not touching his collar. Amazing! What colour hair would our children have, she wondered, and then bit on her tongue to control her wild imagination. Change the subject, quickly, she commanded herself! 'Where do you want the baby to sleep?'

'If you don't mind, perhaps in here with you? It would only be for a few days. I can't believe that Amanda would need longer than that to bring her husband to heel.'

'I don't mind having the baby with me, but you have to understand that I can't possibly stay too long. I have to go to a wedding. My sister Marion is getting married. The last one in the family—except for me, of course.

All the rest of them are married. Would you believe that? Three brothers and two sisters, and they'll all be married. It never ceases to amaze me.'

'Yes, me too,' he said coldly. Katie gave him a sharp look. Something had turned off his smile, left his craggy face with a look of distant reproach. 'So how come you're the only Benedict in the crowd?'

'I don't understand.'

'How come you're not married? I get the impression that all the rest of them are happily settled in Ohio, doing whatever, and here you are, a long way from home, and still not married. How come?'

'I'm not sure that I want to tell you anything about myself,' she said, in equally frigid tones. 'After all, you're just a stranger to me. I'm passing through, so to speak.'

'Ah!' The laughter was back, lurking behind the words, peeping out of those deep blue eyes. 'But since you've already confessed everything to Aunt Grace, and you *are* going to be living in my home, surely you can tell me a little?'

'Well—' She had picked up the baby in her arms, swathed only in a diaper, and was rocking him. The little eyes were blinking, as if the lids were too heavy for them. A few pacing steps would put the lad away, for sure. 'It's not such a big story,' she said softly. 'My dad ran a photographic studio in our home town, and I worked with him. And then he died very suddenly. My mother thought I was too young to run things. Probably she was right. I was only sixteen. She hired a man to run the shop. Jef Stowbridge. And then later, when everyone else except Marion and me had grown up and left home, she married Jef. Only—'

'Only you couldn't get along with your stepfather?'

'Well, yes—but—it's not what you're thinking. Jef is just right for Mom. But he and I didn't see eye to eye about the business, and Mom felt she had to be on his side. I could see that it might cause a split in their marriage—so I just packed my bags and *I* split. That was two years ago and, from what I hear, they're very happy.'

'And you?'

'Well—things didn't work out exactly as I expected. The *Chicago Tribune*, the *Boston Herald*, the papers in Philadelphia, and Baltimore, and Richmond—they just didn't seem to know they needed a photographer fresh out of college, with three cameras and no experience. But I did find a niche, made a living wage, and even had four photographs of my own in a national exhibition last year. It's a living.'

'But you're not wedded to it?'

'No—hardly. I like what I do, but photographers are a dime a dozen, and you have to conform. I hate that word.'

'Me, too,' he said quietly. She had been watching the baby, but his comment brought her head up. He was solemn, appraising. He has something on his mind, she told herself. Something big. Oh well.

He started to say something more, but she stopped him. 'How about hushing up,' she whispered. 'The little fellow's finally asleep. He must have missed a great deal of rest, what with all the newness of things, and his non-stop crying.'

The bed was a Hollywood type, pushed up against one of the walls. She took two pillows and arranged them to make a little pen for him. He was smiling in his sleep. His long blond eyelashes were tightly curled against his cheeks, and his tousled hair hung down over his face in long curls. He reminded her of somebody. Who? The thought escaped her. She bent over the bed to get him properly placed. 'What a waste,' she whispered.

'How so?'

'Look at him. All those curls and eyelashes wasted. He should have been a girl!' She pushed herself back up to standing position, and felt a sudden tension, a touch of fear. Harry King was standing as close to her as a stamp is to the envelope. She tried to back away, but found that her knees were pressed against the side of the bed, and would not answer her command.

'He needs to—to sleep, Mr King,' she stammered. His presence was upsetting her, and she could not tell why. It should have been a pleasure standing beside him. In all Katie's life she had had a fear of standing beside boys. They were always shorter than she, so much so that she had adopted a defensive crouch in the presence of men. But this man towered over her. She had to bend her head back to see his face!

'The name is Harry,' he said quietly. 'Call me Harry. Mr King was my father. You're a cute little rascal, Katie.'

Her head snapped back in astonishment. No one had ever called her that. Well, not since her tenth birthday. Cute little rascal? Did he need glasses? Those blue eyes were close to her—close and staring. It seemed to Katie as if he never blinked. There was a tremor running up and down her legs, something she had never experienced before. He noticed.

'What's disturbing you?' he asked. His deep voice was like a caress, almost as if he were stroking her, hypnotising her. It took a conscious feat of will-power for her to snap out of it.

'I must be tired,' she said. 'I was driving all night. All night.' Her teeth were chattering, and she knew it had nothing to do with missing a night's sleep.

'You know what I like about you?' he asked. And then didn't wait for an answer, just like his aunt. 'I get the feeling that I could kiss you without having to bend over like a pretzel, or break my back doing it. Like this.'

He proceeded to demonstrate. His head moved slowly towards her, trapping her in the pools of his eyes. For a second he hesitated, as a flash of alarm crossed her face, but only for a second. She closed her eyes, trying to wall out the sight of him, and stiffened her will; brought all her defences to bear. And was totally out-manoeuvred.

In the course of her years Katie had been kissed before, on occasion by experts. But with him, something went wrong. His lips feather-touched hers, for just a brief moment of contact, and in that moment some sort of static spark leaped between them, stinging both into the realisation that something extraordinary had happened.

He pulled back from her, leaving her in a puzzled daze, one hand raised to her cheek as if to assure herself that everything was all right. Her eyes opened slowly. He was poised above her, searching her face, a wide grin on his. She tried to move away from him, but again her knees refused the order. He lowered his head again, applying a steadily increasing pressure against her lips until she sighed and opened them to his probing, seeking tongue. Much against her will, her hands encircled his neck, burying themselves in the thick hair at the back of his head. His arms were both around her, pressing her closer against his steel frame. For some reason her leg muscles buckled, throwing her entire weight on to his arms.

He freed one of his hands and it roamed up and down her backbone. She gasped at the fiery touch, and moaned as his hand circled to her breast and hesitated there. Deep in her mind there was an insistent nagging need to get closer to him, but her limp body was beyond her control. She gasped again as the pressure on her mouth increased. The noise disturbed the baby, who whimpered in his sleep, and brought them both back to reality. He lifted his lips from hers, touched the tip of her nose gently, then released her.

With his strength gone from her she collapsed on to the bed, gasping for breath. He had both hands in his pockets now, watching her like a hawk peering down at his next victim. And then, slowly, that wide grin came across his face again. He laughed softly. 'You've got weak knees for this kind of game,' he chortled.

'I don't—I—that's not part of the contract for domestics,' she spluttered. 'I wish you hadn't done that. What will your—what will Eloise say?'

'But we both know that you're not a domestic, don't we?' he returned. 'And as for Eloise, I won't tell her if you won't!'

'Why you—you conniving arrogant—chauvinist!' She spat the words at him, her face flushed with anger. 'You're going to marry Eloise, and you play games with me at the same time?'

'Now, now,' he chuckled. 'You may think I'm going to marry Eloise, and Eloise might think so too, but the truth of the matter is that I'm just not the marrying type.'

'And you think that gives you the right to—to force yourself on me?'

'Come on, love,' he taunted. 'I can't help it if you have weak knees. That was hardly forcing, you know. And don't tell me you didn't enjoy it, because I know you did. I did, too. I would think that my aunt would have picked out a more experienced candidate though. Now, perhaps you'd like to tell me what kind of a plot Aunt Grace is working on this time?

'Coincidence is a little hard to swallow. This road and this house are about as far as you can get from the mainstream of life. Anybody who chose Highway 19W as a short cut to Ohio needs her brain transplanted. It only took me sixty seconds to see that dear Aunt Grace is up to her little game again. And that makes you an accessory to the crime, doesn't it?'

'I haven't the slightest idea what you're talking about!' Katie snapped at him. 'I don't know you, I didn't know your aunt, and I don't even know this poor little kid. Is that all a coincidence?'

'Well, I wouldn't put it past Aunt Grace and my sister to work up some double-barrelled scheme. Don't be alarmed, though. I always manage to uncover the plot before the trap is sprung. Are your bags still out in your car? I'll go get them. You can just sit there and think about what new cover story you plan to tell me, or you can hop across the hall and consult with the First Witch. I'll walk very slowly to give you a better chance.'

'Why you—you insufferable—' But the invective had lost its flavour as the door closed behind him. Just sit here? Why that—insulting man! I'll get down to my car somehow, and I'll—but she had been just sitting, and the inaction did her in. She fell over on her side, feet still on the floor, and dozed away into another fog, forgetfulness.

He returned in about an hour with her three bags. He set them down quietly in the corner, and came over to the bed. With much tender care he picked up her legs and swung them up on the bed. Then, still moving cautiously, he unlaced her high-top brogues and slipped them off. He also loosened the belt of her jeans and brought a blanket from the cupboard to cover her and the baby.

Her wild russet curls had fallen across her eyes and cheek. He brushed them back with a light finger. There was a tiny droplet of perspiration standing on the very tip of her nose. He bent over, and removed it with his tongue. He stood there for another three or four minutes, brooding over her, tracing the outline of her under the blankets, recalling the spark that had jumped between them. It was so obviously another one of Aunt Grace's ploys, yet something didn't feel right, and he was at a loss to say just what it was. He walked back to the door, jingling the change in his pocket with a nervous hand.

'A professional bachelor needs to be very wary indeed,' he muttered to himself as he went out into the corridor. 'Take care, Harry.' But as he wandered down the stairs he wondered if he really wanted to—take care, that is.

CHAPTER THREE

WAKING up had always been a problem for Katie. She did it in stages, unfolding her long slender frame somewhat in the manner of a folding ruler. On this particular morning she faced not only the unfolding problem, but also the fact that she was in a strange bedroom. Both eyes flew open as she struggled to place herself. When recognition struck, she rolled over frantically, searching. 'The baby!' she moaned as her stiff muscles complained. There *had* been a baby. And that monstrous man who thought she was some sort of devil in league with his aunt—Aunt Grace? But there was no baby in sight. A cocoon of blankets and pillows still made a little nest, but it was empty. She rolled back to the edge of the bed and managed to get her feet on the floor.

There was a considerable chatter outside the window, where two bluejays were disputing landing rights on the higher branches of the hickory tree standing close by. Katie checked her watch, then straggled over to look out. There was a delayed reaction. Her watch said eight o'clock, and she was looking eastward, straight into the glare of the sun. 'Good Lord,' she muttered, 'Eight o'clock in the morning?'

Without stopping for shoes she dashed to the door, struggling the while with her jeans, which seemed to have come undone. She stopped to readjust them. Then, assured of some modesty, she pulled the door open, ran barefoot down the stairs, and burst into the kitchen.

'My stars!' Aunt Grace commented from her position at the stove.

'The baby! I can't find the baby,' Katie stammered. 'The baby's gone!'

'Not to worry, my dear. You must have been tired.

You slept so long that Harry took the boy down to the swimming pool. You've slept almost twenty-four hours, girl. And I'm just starting breakfast. Want some?'

'Just coffee,' she muttered, trying to calm herself down. 'Just coffee.' She stumbled over to the kitchen table and dropped heavily into a chair. 'I've never done that before,' she said, 'Not ever in my whole life!'

'Nervous reaction,' Aunt Grace replied. 'You've been living on nerves, my girl. Here, take this coffee and go outside. I'll call you when breakfast is ready.'

Katie cradled the warm mug in her hands, tipped in a tiny splash of milk, and strolled out on to the brick patio behind the kitchen. She moved idly towards the corner of the house, and surveyed the scene. The house was an old Federalist home, of warm, worn brick, with two clapboard wings extending from each side. It was settled near the forward edge of a small plateau, shaped like a stage, looking out over the western valleys and mountains. Behind her, where the backdrop of a stage would be, was an abrupt cliff, shooting almost straight upwards a matter of two hundred feet. In front of her, where the footlights might be, the plateau gently curved around, over a tremendous drop. Only where the bridge crossed the tumbling river, to her left rear, was there any access from the outside. A high wire-mesh fence guarded the lip of the abyss, stretching round to her right until it was blocked from sight behind a small apple orchard.

A nearer clump of trees looked unnatural. A line of poplar trees protected an area from which she could hear Jon squealing. Katie walked quietly across the soft grass until she came upon an Olympic-size swimming pool, surrounded by a concrete apron. The whole pool area was guarded by windbreaking trees, and the water was heated by solar panels. As she walked into the enclosure Jon and Harry squirmed out of the pool, chased each other in the sunlight, and then collapsed on to a pair of wating sun-loungers. Jon saw her almost immediately.

'Momma,' he squealed, wiggled down on to the concrete, and wobbled in her direction. Harry rolled over on his lounger to look up at her. The baby's wobbling was getting out of control. Before he could land back in the pool Katie spurted forward and swept him up. He immediately began to play with the thin gold chain she always wore, communicating in his own private language.

'So, he thinks you're his mother?' Harry called. He stood up and slipped into a robe. Katie could not stop her wandering eyes from inspecting his long lean frame. Big, of course. But slim. Well muscled, with not an ounce of fat to be seen.

'Well, boys his age aren't too perceptive about women,' she returned, as she disengaged a paw from her chain, and offered an ornate button on her blouse in its place. She walked over to where he waited, trying at every step to muster up some conversational *bon mot*. Without effect.

'Where's—Eloise?' she finally managed to get out, cursing herself as soon as she heard the words. Eloise was the last topic she wanted to hear about, not the first. But how does one approach a man at this hour of the morning and say, 'I wish I could run my hands through your hair. Is it really red? Do you honestly mean to marry that harridan, now that I've found you?' Now that I've found you! Get a grip on yourself, Katie Russel, she commanded. I wonder if I could kiss him?

There was no reason to wonder for very long. He closed the distance between them with two leisurely steps, put his hands on her shoulders, around the baby, and kissed her. As before, she could feel the electric shock snap between them as he feathered across her lips. The shock was completely upsetting. She wanted to say and do a million things, but her knees were buckling.

'The baby!' was all she managed to gasp before she collapsed on to her bottom on the concrete apron. He was quick enough, where Jon was concerned. He snatched the child up before Katie hit the ground, and then he stood there, the baby tucked under one arm, and grinned at her. She searched around for a stick or stone to throw at him, but nothing was available.

'Don't stand there and laugh at me,' she snarled up at him. 'It's all your fault. You could have caught me!'

'And dropped the child?' he asked in injured dignity.

He held out his free hand to her, and pulled her back up to her feet. 'Interesting,' he said jovially. 'Does this happen all the time when some man kisses you?'

'No it doesn't!' she raged at him as she tried to brush down her jeans. 'Only when you—' She clamped her hand over her traitorous mouth.

'Only when I do?' he asked. His voice was solemn, but his eyebrows were raised.

'Don't be so conceited,' she snapped. 'It's just that you caught me unawares. I was surprised—I was—'

'I'm sure you were,' he laughed, 'but let's test the theory.' He sat the little boy down on a lounger and concentrated all his attention on her.

'Now then,' he chuckled, 'take notice, little girl. I'm going to kiss you.'

'No! No you're not,' she raged at him. 'I won't— Eloise will see you, and—don't!' His hands were on her shoulders again, drawing her in to the warmth of him, into the golden trap of his arms, and Katie was more afraid than she had ever been in her life. Not of him, but of herself. Tears formed in her green eyes, glistened across her pupils, welled up, and ploughed a wet path down each of her cheeks. 'No,' she pleaded softly. 'Please—no.'

He used a large finger to trap the tears before they dropped off her chin. 'No,' he returned quietly, 'not now.' Moving gently he lifted her up off her feet and sat her down on a chair. And sat silently, watching her.

She licked her lips, tasting the salt of her own tears at one corner, struggling to find something neutral to say. Something that would get him talking, and get his mind off—whatever. Something that would release her from his hypnotic stare. And he was grinning again.

'You said you were an inventor?' she offered. 'You invent things for a living?'

'I believe I do,' he returned. 'You know about inventing?'

'Me? I . . . no, I don't. But it sounds—nice. What do you invent?'

'All kinds of things,' he laughed. 'You're good for my ego, Katie. I thought everybody in the southern states knew Harry King. You haven't a clue, have you?'

'If you mean, do I know about you—I'm sorry, but I don't.'

'You mean the First Witch didn't give you a briefing about me before this plot went into action?'

'Don't talk like that,' she snapped, her face darkening in embarrassment. 'I told you before. I don't know you, I don't know your aunt, and I—why are we having this argument again?' She gulped a deep breath to regain emotional control, then folded her hands in her lap and said primly, 'Tell me about something that you invented.'

'Here. How about this.' From the pocket of his robe he took out a gleaming little screw, and held it up in front of her as if it represented some great triumph.

'You invented this—this screw?' she stammered. 'Nice. Very nice.'

'Nice, very nice,' he mimicked. 'Lady, first of all it's not a screw. It's an aluminum self-tapping, self-locking fastener.'

'Oh. Of course,' she muttered. 'I see that—'

'You don't see a thing,' he laughed. 'Take it.' He dropped the little fastener into her hand. She rolled it over carefully, trying to find something sensible to say about it, but nothing came to mind. It looked like a shiny little screw, no matter what he called it. 'Yes,' she muttered. 'very nice. A fastener? I suppose somebody uses these for something?'

'I believe so,' he returned. 'It's used in the automobile industry these days. In fact, the Big Three auto manufacturers use so many of them that I get a royalty of about five cents on every car they manufacture.'

'My goodness,' she sighed, fumbling around in her head for the arithmetic which had always been her downfall at school. 'And how many cars do they make for your five cents apiece?'

'Last year was a bad year,' he laughed. 'They only made five million. This year I hope to do better.'

'My, that's very nice,' she commented, and then her mind caught up to one or two misplaced decimal points. 'Oh! That's two hundred and fifty thousand dollars!'

'Give or take a few thousand,' he laughed. 'You are a quick one.'

'And you'll make the same every year?'

'Well no, hardly. This country has about fifty thousand people who make their living by inventing things. They're pretty good at arithmetic, too. So about the end of next year there will be somebody who will make a basic improvement on my little baby here, and the scramble will start all over again. It keeps us on our toes, so to speak.'

All the time he had been talking about his little fastener his face had been alight with a glow that made him look—boyish, Kate thought. He's really interested in this thing! But now, the glow and the grin were gone, the eyes a little more flinty, the tone more sarcastic.

'And now that you've had a night to think about it,' he asked casually, 'what's your new cover story?'

'Cover story?'

'Yes. You know. What tale have you and Aunt Grace cooked up about yourself, now that the first one didn't take?'

'I'm—not sure I like what you're saying,' she responded. Her voice was prim and placid, but there were sparks deep in her eyes, sparks of anger. 'Your aunt had nothing to do with me. I am a photographer. I don't mind staying around for a few days to help with the baby, but when my car is fixed I'm going to Ohio for a wedding. Just as soon as my car is fixed!'

'That's a tough act,' he chuckled. 'You would have done better to stick to something simple like housekeeping. So you're a photographer, huh? And what do you intend to photograph around here?'

'Well, I don't need to photograph anything around here,' she fumbled. 'I didn't mean to wind up in this valley at all. I was just passing through. One of my friends in Charlotte recommended this route, and I just sort of followed along. But if I have to wait for my car to be fixed, I—'

'You do,' he said solemnly. 'It will take some time. So what would you like to photograph?'

'I don't know,' she said musingly. 'I don't know the area. But I do love that skyline over there. Is it possible to get up on the top of this mountain behind us, so I could make a panorama of the mountains? That would be nice. And then maybe a historical point or two. Do you know the history of these parts?'

'Wow,' he commented, shaking his head. 'We can get you up to a place where you can make your panorama. About the rest of it, we'll see. When would you like to go?'

'Well, it has to be done in the morning, with the sun behind me. How about today. Right now?'

'I don't see why not,' he said casually. He stood up again, and offered his hand. She felt a need to touch him. To walk back to the house with him, hand in hand. He pulled her up to her feet. She was looking over his shoulder directly at the kitchen door, and saw something moving there. Eloise had finally got up. And at the very moment of recognition he swung Katie around, pressing her hard up against his full length, and captured her lips in a tide of passion that made everything which preceded it seem like so much innocent child's play. The pressure, the mindless pressure, kept on and on, until she was shaking in every limb, and gasping for breath. Then he released her and walked away, chortling, with Jon in his arms.

Katie staggered, reached out a hand for support, and slumped on to the lounge chair again. He was whistling and Jon was gurgling as the two of them went up to the house. The kitchen door opened, and Eloise came out, just as they arrived. Eloise positioned herself directly in front of them as Harry set the baby down on its feet, and the pair embraced before they disappeared through the door.

'Why you—you conceited, double-dealing skunk,' Katie muttered as she staggered to her feet and started up the walk. 'Why you double-dyed pig-stealing—con-niving—man! I ought to put a gypsy curse on you—or an Indian curse, there's the thing! Paleface talks with forked tongue!' And then, using her best imitation of a Hollywood Indian dance, she shuffled a circular path in the grass and called out, 'Oh Great Manitou, send the red-headed white man a—' A what? A broken arm? A slippery tongue? Or—'a case of boils!' She was still laughing at herself when she stumbled into the kitchen and fell into a chair, holding her aching sides. And immediately smothered it all in the face of Aunt Grace's stern mien.

'So,' the older woman said seriously, 'you've got the powers! It's not a nice thing, though, to send a curse on Harry. He really means well, you know.'

'Sure he does,' Katie returned sarcastically. 'But he deserves every bit of it. Every bit!'

'That's true,' Aunt Grace replied, 'but if we gave men everything they deserve, where would we women be? Maybe you could make it just a tiny set of boils?'

Katie grinned up at her affectionately. 'Surely you don't believe in all that, do you?' she asked. 'That went out at the turn of the century.'

'Not in the mountans. There's more than one who still believes. More than one. I can still remember Granny

Sills, down Greasy Cove way. She was a witch without a doubt. And a herb woman. Carried all those herbs of hers around in a black reticule, and not a person would cross her for fear of the "eye", you know. Do you know about herbs, Katherine?'

'Oh yes. My great-grandmother was a gypsy. And my grandmother coached me in the remedies for years. Some of the simple ones did a lot of good, and, lacking anything else, they all had some uses. Or maybe I should say they did no harm. You don't have a herb garden?'

'No, I don't. Nothing.'

'But you've got the beginnings. There are plenty of dandelions out there in the lawn, and there's a sassafras down by the swimming pool. That's a pair of good starters.'

'What's a good starter?' Harry had come back into the kitchen, carrying Jon on his shoulders. Eloise crowded close behind him, her sultry curves draped closely in a crimson cat-suit. All at once Katie realised that she was still wearing the dirty, crumpled, smelly set of jeans and shirt in which she had started her journey from Charlotte. A combination which she had worn now for over thirty-six wrinkled hours!

'Breakfast is a good starter,' Katie mumbled. 'I have to go and change.' She tried to slide around them, to get out the door.

'But breakfast is ready for the table,' Aunt Grace wailed.

'Leave her alone,' Harry ordered, in a tone that made Katie wish she had the nerve to whack him as she went by. 'The girl positively reeks. Out you go, little Miss Russel. But hurry. The chariot leaves in fifteen minutes.'

She sidled by him nervously, and stopped long enough to stick out her tongue at his massive back. It was apparent that he had eyes in the back of his head. Before she could escape out into the hall, one of those massive hands swung around and bounced smartly off the curve of her bottom, adding more force than necessary to her flight.

He was waiting for her at the far side of the house when she came out, stuffed by the triple breakfast she had snatched. Eloise's back could be seen as she wiggled her way down to the pool. 'Jon is staying with Aunt Grace,' he reported. 'My, that's really a load. Is your lunch in there?'

'No,' she snarled at him, 'it's my cameras. What did you expect, a Polaroid?'

'Well, to tell you the truth, that's just what I did expect,' he laughed. 'What do you have in that big case?'

'It's a converted war-surplus Hasselblatt,' she told him, slipping back the canvas cover from the huge barrel of the camera. 'My father bought it and converted it. The only trouble with it is that it weighs a whole bunch of pounds.'

He was impressed. His eyes said so, and his grin. Finally he was impressed. He relieved her of the burden, stowing the Hasselblatt and her three lightweight SLRs in the back seat. As he helped her up into the high seat of the four-wheel-drive Jeep he said softly, 'Could it be that I've been mistaken about you, little girl?'

'Don't call me that,' she snapped back at him. 'I'm not some sort of baby!' She shook her arm free. He stood by the side of the vehicle for a moment, rocking back and forth on his heels, his face displaying the picture of his mind at work.

'Not necessarily,' he announced to the wide world. Then, without explanation, he walked around to the driver's seat and started the engine.

The little wooden bridge grumbled under their wheels as the Jeep rolled across. Katie leaned out far enough to see the little stream, some twenty feet down, that had carved the gorge.

'It's all limestone rock around here,' he yelled at her. 'That creek's been working at it for hundreds of years.

Makes into a fine waterfall a little way down. Some time, if you're interested, we'll take a look at it!'

Once out on the highway, heading up and eastward, she huddled close to the door, determined to absorb as much of the mountain scenery as possible. They were in a world of variegated greens. A few clumps of tall white pine and oak stood out from the smaller poplar, spruce, wild apple, and oak. And all around them, in patches that seemed to stretch for acres, were the closely interwoven laurel bushes. 'In most places they're so close that you can't get through without an axe,' he yelled. 'This was once the real forest primeval, but a massive forest fire destroyed most everything. What you see is secondary growth, mostly. Like it?'

She answered with a smile, savouring the fragrance of the pine. Occasionally they passed open meadows, and dirt trails, but no sign of houses. But the pull of the mountain glades could not fight back her major interest. Out of the corner of her eyes she watched him. He had pushed his sleeves up to the elbow, and held the wheel lightly, his corded muscles flicking corrective actions as the road curled and weaved upward. His hair sparkled in the sunlight, showing gold flecks among the red. He whistled as he drove, carefree, looking younger than— whatever his years were. It was altogether a pleasant thing, watching him, she thought. Gradually her head turned, until she was staring, devouring him with her eyes. Her lips parted, with her tongue slightly protruding as she concentrated. She was so engrossed that she hardly noticed they had swung off the paved highway, and were following a dirt track through an open meadow, pointing straight ahead towards a clump of rock and woodland that rose higher than the flat area in which they were driving. He braked the Jeep, set the handbrake, and turned to her.

'From here on,' he laughed, 'it's shank's mare, lady.' He pointed to where the trail they were following split in three directions. 'We take the left-hand bend.'

'Okay,' she sighed, thinking of the weight of the big camera. 'Where do the other two go?'

'The middle one leads on to Business Ridge, towards Devil's Creek Gap,' he said. 'The other one is the Appalachian Trail. You know about that, I guess?'

'No, I guess I don't. Should I?'

'I would think so,' he commented drily. 'It's a hiking trail that follows the higher ridges of the Appalachian Mountains, all the way from the centre of Maine to North Georgia. About two thousand miles, I would guess. It has rest areas and hostels along the route, and only one major gap, up in New York, where the Hudson River carved a mighty hole in the mountain chain. We must try it some time.'

'Two thousand miles? I—I don't think I can spare the time. Especially if I have to carry these cameras.'

'So I'll help,' he chuckled. He climbed out, reached back for her heaviest camera case, and started up the trail. She slid out of her seat as fast as she could, fumbled at the straps of her lighter cameras and her supply case, and hurried after him.

'Hey wait,' she was finally forced to call. He stopped in mid-stride and glanced back at her. She thought he was about to say something sarcastic. Instead his eyes lit up, that wide grin swept across his face, and he slowed his pace.

'It's called Flat Top Mountain,' he announced grandly when they reached their destination. 'Because it's flat, of course. And behind us, that's Big Bald. Straight ahead and down is Business Ridge. The town on the other side is Erwin, the biggest city in Unicoi Country. We'll go there one day.'

'Yes. Nice,' she muttered as she struggled to assemble her folding tripod, and set the camera up. It was about an hour before the sun would be overhead, so she had a clear view ahead, into the valley of the Tennessee. 'It looks like an ocean of waves, all fixed in place,' she called to him. 'What am I looking at?'

'You're on top of the Smokey Mountains here,' he returned. 'Ahead of you are a whole series of smaller ranges, running generally from north-east to south-west. In between each of those ranges is a little river which generall runs south until it joins a larger river, and then eventually into the Tennessee. They tell that in the old days every spring brought floods and destruction. In the 1930s the Federal government organised a public corporation, the TVA, and gave it the job of stopping the floods and producing cheap electricity. They built more dams than I can count, and it all worked. There hasn't been a flood in my lifetime. How about that?'

She was busy at her tripod, tightening the clamps on the legs, and paying only partial attention. 'Nice,' she said.

'That your favourite word?'

She stopped, flustered, only half aware of what she had said. 'Hmm?'

'Oh don't mind me,' he chuckled. 'I'm just going to sit back and watch woman at work. I believe in the equality of the sexes.'

'I'll just bet you do,' she muttered, as she stripped the cover from the old camera and positioned it on the tripod. It locked into its holder with a satisfying click. She wiped off the universal joint with a fresh tissue, and experimentally swung the long nose of the Hasselblatt round, one eye on the viewfinder.

'My great-great-grandfathers settled all this,' he said contentedly. 'Came into the empty land, and made a nation out of it. Right over there where Elizabethtown is now. They're called the over-mountain men. That's where it all started.'

Her eye was busy picking out the sequence of pictures she wanted to take for the panorama, looking for the landmarks that would be the margins of each shot, the place where the next shot would overlap. The magazine was already loaded, and she began at the northern edge of the area.

'Up there, was it?' she muttered, concentrating on her work. The shutter snapped. Her hands went about their business automatically. 'Funny, I thought a whole nation of Indians lived in this land.' She snapped a second exposure of the same area, just to be sure, and moved the camera on its gimbals to the next scene.

'Never believe it,' he laughed. 'They all lived south of here.'

She looked away from the viewfinder to look at him. That lazy infectious grin was wide on his face. 'And they never came up here?' she asked.

'Oh sure they did,' he said. 'Hunting. That's different than living. Our people came into the land, leased five million acres from the Cherokees, made a treaty of eternal peace, and settled down.'

She was back at the camera again, hunting scenic effects. 'Nice,' she commented. 'So what's the first thing they did after that?'

'Like I said, they settled in. They built a fort, and began farming. Brought the whole land under cultivation finally. It took a long time, of course. Had to get rid of the buffalo first. You can't raise crops in buffalo country. They trampled everything.'

By this time her camera had traversed the full width of the panorama that she wanted. She marked up her record-pad, covered the lens, and turned around to him. He was squatting on his heels at the end of the clearing, a long thin blade of grass between his teeth.

'Let me get this straight,' she chuckled. 'You came into the valleys, swore a treaty of eternal peace and promptly built a fort? Against whom?'

'Now, wait a minute,' he protested. 'We built a fort against the—well—the Indians did raid the settlements, you know.'

'Of course they did,' she retorted. 'Was that before or after you killed all their buffalo? Which came first, the chicken or the egg? Did they raid you because you built the fort, or did you build the fort because they raided you?'

'Boy, are you some kind of a country lawyer,' he snorted. He got up and walked over to her, dropping those huge hands on her shoulders again, drawing her up against him. 'I can see there's only one way to keep you subdued, girl.' And once again her sight was blotted out as his head shadowed her, his lips caressed her with a gentle touch, and Katie's world came unglued. Minutes later, still clinging to him desperately, she managed to get her wind back.

'That's a terrible way to avoid a logical argument,' she sighed.

They finished up their efforts by eleven-thirty, packed up the equipment, and hiked back to the Jeep. The strain of the hike, after a year or more in city ways, left Katie tired. Harry loaded the equipment into the back of the vehicle. She sat quietly in the passenger seat, watching. When he finally came around to the driver's seat, she stared at him.

'You're not a bit winded, are you?' she asked.

'No. Not really. But you did surprise me, girl.'

'Surprise you? How?'

'I would have sworn you didn't know a camera from a sow's belly. And instead you looked very professional about it all!'

'Damn you, Harry King!' Her ire was up, but she was too tired to hit him, as logic dictated. 'Is that what it was? A test of my cover story?'

'Got it in one, lady,' he laughed, as he started the motor. 'Only the results are confusing. I may have to run some other tests.'

'Smart alec,' she grumbled, turning her attention to the side of the road. 'Hey! Stop!' The brakes squealed as he jammed them on forcefully. The vehicle skidded, raised a cloud of dust, and slid to a stop. By this time Katie was entangled with the metal post of the windscreen, struggling to hang on, coughing out dust from her beclouded lungs.

'Are you all right?' He swept her into his arms and began a detailed check.

'I'm all right,' she gasped, 'Or I would be if you would stop pawing me! I just saw something.'

'Well, it better be important,' he told her sternly. 'I almost put us both through the glass, girly. What was it?'

'There!' She gestured toward a low area where run-off from Flat Top had made what was almost a swamp. 'There. That flower with the shiny green leaves. See it?'

'I don't see any flower.'

'Well, of course not. It's too late in the season for the flower. But you can see the plant. I've got to get some. I haven't seen cinquefoil in years.' She scrambled from the Jeep and began harvesting the plants, roots and all. He watched her, stunned. When she had filled her pockets, her extra camera case, and a paper bag that had been lying in the back of the vehicle, she came back, her face ashine with discovery.

He was sitting at the wheel, watching, as she climbed back in. 'You're a funny one,' he said softly. She looked quickly at him, holding her breath.

'I'm not sure that I will ever get you figured out,' he continued. 'I just get adjusted to the idea that you really are a photographer, and you start playing flower-girl on me. What gives?'

'I don't know,' she said softly, trying to keep laughter out of her voice. 'Your first opinion still might have been right. How do you know that the pictures weren't over-exposed, or something?'

He shook his head, but there was a sparkle in those deep blue eyes, as if his always-churning mind had found a new path to explore. He stared at her for a matter of minutes, then started the motor and they moved off.

The trip down the mountain was made in silence, he concentrating on his driving, she relaxed in her seat, eyes half-closed, admiring the mountain scenery as it unfolded; absorbing the caw of the blackbirds; admiring the hawk wheeling high overhead in the late August sun.

'They came for your car,' he noted, as he swung off the highway into the parking area. She opened both eyes and looked around. Her battered little VW was gone.

'How long will it take to fix it?' she asked eagerly.

'Can't say,' he returned as he piloted the Jeep across the bridge and up beside the house. 'I'll call the garage and see what they have to say.'

'Please ask them to hurry,' she pleaded timidly. 'I really do have to get to Ohio. My sister will kill me if I'm late for her wedding.'

'I thought you wanted to take some more pictures?'

'I—well—they aren't important. Unless we could do them tomorrow?'

'No, I'm afraid not. I have to run over to Knoxville tomorrow. I'm working on a problem for the State, and I have to report in.'

'The day after?'

'Maybe. Don't worry about it. I'm just as anxious as you are to get you out of my house. I laughed when I first saw you. You make a lousy conspirator. But the longer I know you—well, maybe you do better at it than I imagined. Don't worry, little girl, the sooner you're out of here, the better I'll feel.'

'And that goes double for me,' she shouted after his disappearing back. She leaned back in the seat, waiting for her inner storms to dissipate. What in the world have you come to, Katie Russel, she lectured herself. All he has to do is press a button and you shoot off like a sky-rocket. What happened to easy-going dependable Miss Russel, the one who could shoulder all kinds of problems and remain cool? Where is she? Or was she ever? Is this the real me, a sarcastic, raving harridan?

There was only one thing for sure: although she really didn't want to leave, the only way to preserve sanity was to shake the dust of this place off her feet, and move out as fast as she could. She shook her head in disgust, the heavy curls bouncing down over her eyes. 'Just get me my car,' she muttered after Harry, 'and I'll show you the fastest retreat the world has ever seen!'

Wearily she edged herself out of the vehicle, slung her collection of cameras and bags over her shoulder, and struggled around to the back of the house. I've got to get myself rested and organised, she told herself. But it just wasn't her day. As she came around the house she ran into Eloise.

'Excuse me,' she muttered as she almost knocked the smaller woman off her feet.

'Hey, wait!' Eloise called after her. 'Wait!'

With all her might Katie wanted to continue, to run into the kitchen, up the stairs, and slam the door of her room behind her. But courtesy demanded she wait. She did.

'I need to have a talk with you,' Eloise began. Her high, lilting voice set Katie's teeth on edge.

'I don't have the time right this minute,' she compromised. 'I've got film in these cameras that I must get out. Later?'

'Of course,' the other woman returned. 'Later will be fine. But do let me thank you for keeping my fiancé entertained this morning. In some ways he's like a little boy, and I was just too busy to do anything with him. He's a dear boy, of course, but wearying.'

'Yes, of course,' Katie muttered, ducking through the kitchen door. And then, when she was sure she could not be heard, 'But you'd better buy a ball and chain for your *fiancé* before he gets loose among the chickens!'

The kitchen was empty. There was a note chalked up on the wallboard that served for family announcements. 'Lunch is cold-cuts, in the refrigerator,' it said. 'Jon and I have gone to Erwin for supplies.' Which at least gives me a breathing spell, and maybe time for a nap, she told herself. Strange, that I could sleep for twenty-four hours, and still need a nap!

She snatched a sandwich, and had one foot on the

second stair when she heard his voice through the half-closed door of the study. He was talking on the telephone. She crossed her fingers against the bad luck, and shamelessly stopped to listen.

'Look, George,' he said. 'I understand what you're telling me. She ran the engine without any oil, and all the cylinders are seized up. Yes, I understand that the engine is a pile of junk and will have to be replaced. Yes. A rebuilt engine will be fine. Yes, I know you keep them in stock, and could change one in—how long? Two hours? Oh, my God! Yes, I understand. I'm proud of you, George. Now listen. It's going to take you at least two weeks to find the right engine for that car. That's what I said. Two weeks. No, you can't do it tomorrow. Two weeks. George, you'd better get this right. We've been friends for twenty-five years. Two weeks, you hear!'

Katie's mind told her that she should be angry. That she should storm into the room and accuse him of—of trying to maroon her in his mountains. But her mind had no control over her body. Instead of rushing down the hall and beating him about the head and shoulders, her feet carried her quietly up to her room, where she fell on to the bed and almost immediately dropped off to sleep again. Whatever it was she dreamt that afternoon, she could never recall, but when he peeped in the door an hour later he was surprised to see a beautiful wide smile on her face.

CHAPTER FOUR

At four-thirty Katie managed to break free from her sleep spell. In the magical way things seemed to happen in this house, Jon was beside her, just waking up himself. She luxuriated in the comfort as she cuddled, dressed, and changed the baby. When they finally came downstairs everyone else was in the kitchen. Harry was standing by the open back door, holding his arm up to the light. Eloise was sitting at the table, smoking. The number of butts crushed in her saucer indicated she had been at it for some time. Aunt Grace was busy at the oven.

'And if it isn't our honoured guest!' Katie had almost forgotten how shrill and penetrating Eloise's voice was. She cringed away from the comment.

'Don't fool around with that one,' Harry said. 'She's a genuine grade-A photographer.'

'No, and you'd better not, neither,' Aunt Grace interrupted. 'Don't go funnin' this girl. She's got the powers. You be careful!'

'I'm not funning her,' he laughed. 'Got the powers, has she? We'd better step carefully around here. Damn, I wish I knew what's happened to my arm.' He rolled his sleeve up to the elbow.

'Boils!' Aunt Grace told him. There was a touch of glee in her voice. She looked at Katie and briefly winked an eye. 'You have boils, Harry.'

'Now how in the world could I get boils?' he protested worriedly. 'I haven't been into anything, or eaten anything strange. It could be that cat of yours, Eloise.'

'What do you think, Katie?' asked Aunt Grace. 'Did your gypsy great-grandmother pass along any sovereign remedies?'

Katie strolled over to the door into the sunlight, little Jon riding on her hip. There was an eruption of small blisters in the crease of Harry's elbow, and she recognised it at a glance. Contact dermatitis, probably something carried on the fur of the cat.

'It certainly looks like boils to me,' she commented. 'There is an old gypsy remedy, but I suppose it wouldn't work on you. Herb cures only work for those who believe in them, you know.'

'Don't give me that,' he retorted. There was a look of real concern on his face. Good Lord, Katie thought, he's sensitive to this sort of thing! One minute he's the domineering mountain man, the next a very worried boy!

'All right,' she soothed, 'we'll do something about it. Aunt Grace, do you have any of that plain old yellow laundry soap?'

'Got a lot of it,' the older woman replied. She was having difficulty avoiding outright laughter. 'Nobody uses it nowadays, that's how come we have a lot left over. What do we do?'

'First Harry scrubs his arm with it. Gently, of course. Then Eloise minds the baby while I go back upstairs to get something.'

'Not me!' Eloise waved her off. 'The only reason you could find to hang around here is as a baby-sitter. Don't try to pawn that brat off on me. A baby-sitter! Is that the best you can do?'

'It's an honest trade,' Katie said truculently. 'Can you say the same for yours?' The light of battle was sparking in her green eyes. The little blonde drew back, as if expecting a physical assault. That's what I ought to do, Katie told herself. I ought to punch her in the mouth. And stomp her a couple of times. I've had enough of this Goodie Two-Shoes business!

Harry interrupted the incipient war. 'I'm about to die from boils,' he lamented. 'At least you could hold the baby, Eloise.'

'All right, all right,' the blonde conceded. As soon as

she transferred the child, Katie made a dash for her room. In the corner on a chair she found her jacket, and under it the paper bag she had filled on the mountain. She raced back down the stairs two at a time.

'We need a heavy saucepan,' she dictated, as she dumped the roots and leaves of the cinquefoil plant into the metal sink and began washing off the dirt. 'Normally this material should be dried. It's strong that way. But for now, stick that in the pan and boil it in about two cups of water, Aunt Grace. Give it about thirty minutes on the boil, then soak a clean soft cloth in it and lay it over the boils. Oh, bruise those leaves. That will help to release the strength of it. And do it again just before you go to bed, Harry.'

'Excellent,' Harry said in a very self-satisfied tone. 'While it's boiling, Katie, let me show you around my land.'

'But Harry,' Eloise shrilled. 'We were going to talk, you and I. You said—'

'Yes, you're right. We will,' he answered softly. 'While the two witches are gathered around the boiling cauldron here. Come on, we'll duck into the library.'

Katie stepped back out of the way as he shepherded Eloise out of the kitchen. As he went by he leaned over and whispered in her ear, 'I see that you and Aunt Grace had a conference this afternoon. How's the conspiracy coming?'

She tried to dredge up an answer, but only managed to sputter, 'Oh—you—you' before he had gone out the door. For some reason she felt—disappointed. A cloud settled over her mind, a cloud of dismal proportions. And it lasted until she had served the supper, bathed and bedded the baby, and turned in herself.

Whatever cloud it was that hung over the house that night, by the early morning of the next day at least Harry was back to normal. He came down to the kitchen, where Katie was feeding Jon, and he was whistling.

'Better hurry up, girl,' he chided her, patting her

well-rounded bottom for emphasis. 'The sun waits for no—ah—woman, that is, and I'm off to Atlanta. Is my breakfast ready?' Without waiting for an answer he pulled out a chair at the table, thumped himself down, and buried himself in the folds of the *Erwin Record*.

'You could help,' she stuttered, amazed at her own temerity. It was a question she would never have dared raise back home with her brothers.

'Oh?' he queried, lowering the paper.

'Well, you could feed the baby for example, while I cook for everybody else. And then I have to clean the kitchen, lay out the supper, and start the laundry!'

'Complaints, complaints,' he laughed. 'Is that all you've got to do, woman? That's all I hear around here. Complaints!'

'You really are a male chauvinist, Harry King,' she muttered under her breath as she started to scramble half-a-dozen eggs in the big skillet. He chuckled at her, put down his newspaper, and started to play the 'into the hangar' game that seemed to be the only way to get food down Jon's throat.

Eloise showed up at seven-thirty, dressed in a sleek green suit, with a suede jacket to match.

'I have to finish feeding the baby,' Harry chortled at her, 'and then clean myself up.'

'Take your time,' the blonde woman offered. 'I just want a cup of coffee, and a few words with Katie, while you do that. We'll go out on the patio.'

'Oh, we will?' Kate muttered under her breath, but Harry was staring at her. He nodded her towards the door. So even though she didn't want to go, she followed Eloise out on to the flagstones, and took an adjacent chair at her signal.

'Katie,' she said, adjusting her skirts to fall neatly, but not looking up at all, 'Harry and I—well, as you know, we're going to Atlanta for the weekend, as we usually do. But before we leave, I thought—well, to tell the truth—Harry asked me to tell you a few things.'

'Harry asked you?'

'Of course. Last night, late, in my room. You surely are aware that Harry and I are a team? Or are you so young that— no, that can't be. How old are you?'

'Twenty-four.'

'I see. And a very young twenty-four at that, I imagine. Well, Harry is thirty-two, and I'm thirty. And while thirty-two is a nice age for a man, thirty is a death-wish for an actress. It's a young woman's game. I started in New York, dropped to Chicago, and now all the work I can get is in Atlanta. After this, I'm only one step from oblivion. You understand?'

'I understand the words,' Katie said frankly, 'but not the intent. Come out with it. What do you want to tell me?'

'All right.' Eloise laughed that shrill trill that set Katie's teeth on edge. 'Straight. Every girl needs a security blanket. Harry's mine. He belongs to me. He's a great friend, and a fine lover, but he has this continuous need to fool around. So until I get him to the altar, I have to overlook his playful little interludes. I don't want you to misunderstand, though. He may give you a whirl, or a one-night stand in his bed, but he always comes back to me!' The blonde took a deep breath, emphasising her tremendous figure, smoothing down her blouse with trailing fingers to add punctuation to the declaration.

'Harry's an all-American boy,' she continued. 'I know what he likes, and I've got it. 38D, my dear.'

'I—I'm not in competition,' Katie stuttered, her mind a whirl of confusion. 'I'm just here to mind the baby.' Would Harry have done that? Asked Eloise to brush her off? Why not, she thought. He's half-boy, half-man. Maybe he would look for somebody to do his dirty work for him.

'If you are sure you can keep that at the front of your mind we'll have no trouble,' Eloise snapped. 'Better still, we'll be gone until Monday. Why don't you get into your little car and be on your way before we get back!'

With that statement Eloise got up gracefully and walked back to the kitchen.

Katie watched her go, measuring the swing of her hips, the set of her shoulders, and feeling a gnawing pain originating in the pit of her own stomach. It's hard enough to be second-rank, but to have it thrown in your face like that? Lord, what must he think of me? They are lovers, those two. And somewhere in the middle of their lovemaking they had talked—and laughed?—about Katie Russel. Poor Katie Russel. We mustn't let her get hurt by it all, must we? He belongs to Eloise and surely, sooner or later, they'll get married! The knife twisted in her wound, and she struggled without hope to master this new feeling, this wild regret. How can you lose something you never had? For a brief moment panic ruled, and then was put down.

'No one can hurt you when you are part of the land and the sky,' Grandmother always preached. With leaden steps Kate got up, walked across the patio, and out on to the lush grass of the lawn. She threw herself down flat on her back, settled her hips comfortably, and forced her eyes to watch the parade of fluffy clouds that marched across the sky. Her hands scrabbled at the ends of the blue-green grass. Then gradually she commanded her muscles to relax, and they obeyed. Her stomach slowly ceased to churn, her thoughts cleared as the cloud motion hypnotised her, and she found a fragmentary peace.

An hour later she heard the noise of the car leaving, and a few minutes after that the tentative wobbles of Jon's steps as someone let him out the back door. 'Katie? Where are you?'

She raised herself to sitting position, pivoted, and waved to Aunt Grace, still standing in the doorway. Jon squealed as his eyes focused on her, and he increased his speed. She opened her arms to receive him.

'Katie?' Aunt Grace came a little way out on to the patio. 'Harry's boils have almost disappeared, Katie!

You would have thought he invented that poultice himself!' All of which was news enough to dream on, and that night she did.

The weekend passed slowly, almost as if it were a slow-motion movie. On Saturday morning Aunt Grace drove her down into Erwin, to buy a few sundries for her wardrobe, a playpen for Jon, and a month's supply of disposable diapers and skin cream.

'I used to go on to Johnson City,' Aunt Grace told her as they started back. 'But now the downtown shopping is dead, and the highways are loaded with mile after mile of malls and shopping centres. I hate it.'

'It's happening everywhere,' Katie said, trying to bring a little comfort. 'You should see Cleveland. Do you suppose we could stop at the garage and check on my car?'

'No, I don't think so,' Aunt Grace said very quickly. 'They close on Saturdays, it's a religious holiday, and Harry said if I let you within ten miles of that garage he'd have my scalp!'

'Well! He's a—very arrogant fellow,' Katie snapped.

'Yes. Indeed he is!' But the older woman was giggling, and Katie found it impossible not to join in.

The rest of the day was a leisurely rest. Jon was particularly tractable, especially after Kate dumped him into the swimming pool, and let him exhaust himself until naptime. August had slipped into September, and cool winds were blowing, but the shelter of the trees, and the solar heating, kept the pool a centre of enjoyment.

On Sunday they all got up early enough to attend a church service at the Central Baptist Church in Erwin. The rest of the day drifted by, filled with the cool fingers of pine-scented breeze from off the mountain behind the house.

Sunday night was interminably long. She had managed to get Jon to sleep in his new playpen in the corner of her room, but could not settle herself. It was a dark night. The sun had set within a halo of clouds, and the moon was not due to appear until late. A sprinkle of stars distinguished the blow of the sky from the heavy loom of the mountains. She leaned her elbows on the windowsill, cupped her chin in her palms, and dreamed.

The crickets were particularly loud this evening, and from high on the mountain came the howl that spelled bobcat. There was an aura of—waiting—about the night, but Katie was so deep in dreams that she could not pinpoint the source. She was waiting for the sound of wheels, for the return of that arrogant conceited man! She shrugged off the thought, and went back to her contemplation of the night. Little Katie, she told herself, all alone in the universe.

There was the brief piping of a nightingale's song from the orchard, interrupted by the haunting call of a diesel locomotive, hurrying coal-loaded cars from the mines of West Virginia to the power plants of North Carolina.

Unable to conceal her laughter, and afraid she might wake the baby, she gave thought to something else— anything else—to do. The answer came on the caress of a tiny breeze, penetrating through to her conscience. The swimming pool! It was after eleven o'clock at night. Nothing stirred. The fact that she had no bathing suit with her was hardly a drawback, for there was no one to see.

She stripped off the little sun-dress she had worn all day, and changed her shoes for rubber clogs. She snatched up two of the huge red towels from her bathroom, and a warm robe, and stole downstairs and out to the edge of the pool. Not even a whisper of a breeze penetrated the guardian trees that surrounded the pool. She stretched up on her toes, shedding her robe, and as she did so the moon made its first appearance over the eastern ridges. Its silver light re-cast her from an ordinary mortal to a poised silver goddess. She tingled in the light, shed her utilitarian briefs, wrapped her toes over the edge of the concrete apron, and dived deep into the warm waiting waters.

It was like receiving a velvet welcome. Freshly fed from the mountain stream that meandered across the meadow, but constantly warmed by the solar collectors and electrical heaters, it lacked the overpowering sting of chlorination that destroys the enjoyment of most pools. She came up half-way down the pool, and coasted to the end with three or four powerful breast strokes. She shook the water from her hair and face, poised with feet flat against the wall of the pool, took a deep breath, and plunged in an Australian crawl, her legs churning the water like a paddle wheel. So intent was she on her goal that she did not hear the noises at the poolside.

After six laps at full speed, she had had enough. She coasted the last few feet to the deepest end and, using her forward momentum, vaulted up and out, to stand dripping on the concrete. She had landed again in the pool of moonlight, feeling exhilarated, reaching back into her primeval past to become one with nature.

She turned back to the edge of the pool, a silver sprite, curling her toes again over the edge of the apron and leaning slightly forward. And then froze in startled shock as two huge masculine hands wrapped themselves around her from the rear, treasuring her tiny breasts and pulling her back against the hard masculine figure behind her.

The shock was momentary, her reaction instant. Without a pause to enquire she pulled herself forward into a shallow racing dive, and hit the water with a splash, tipping the man behind her into the pool. The hands slackened their grip almost instantly. She used the moment to race away to the shallow end of the pool, barely escaping his clutching fingers. No sooner had she hurtled herself out of the water than the man, fully clothed, managed the same feat.

'Now that was a devil of a thing to do,' Harry King mourned at her. 'Look at my new suit!' He was busy stripping it from him before she could make up her mind what to do next. Her mind said run! Surely no man with his trousers half off could catch a woman who wore only moonbeams? But her body disregarded the order. Her own body held her in thrall, prisoner to the rapidly denuded male figure, whose every attractive inch sparkled in the moonlight.

'Well, you deserved it,' she snapped at him. 'You—you're like an octopus, Harry King. And what are you doing here? You're supposed to be in Atlanta with Eloise!' Her eyes swivelled wildly, spotting the towels she had dropped. Her feet carried her in their direction. He followed, snatching one of them up before she could claim it for protection.

'But I'm not, and you're glad,' he returned. 'You've been sitting up waiting for me to come back, and here I am. Lucky you!'

'Lucky me?' she squeaked. 'I never had it so good, caught out with a man with no clothes on? Just what in the world do you think you're doing, Mr King?' It was hard to keep her voice cool and decisive. Especially since he had picked up the other towel and was advancing on her.

'Why, I'm just drying you off,' he said solemnly. 'Why do you always put the worst possible interpretation on everything I do?' He had completely enveloped her now, wrapping her tightly in the huge red towel, and sealing her in with the strength of his arms. For just a moment she relaxed, pleased beyond words to be in that shelter. And then her conscience began to niggle at her, and she tried to fight her way out.

'Hey,' he laughed, 'calm down. I'm only drying you off.' And it was true that his hands were gently rubbing her down, through the heavy fibre of the towel. But there were too many gaps where the towel did not fit, and where his hands continued to wander.

'Stop that! At once!' she hissed at him. 'At once!'

'Of course,' he said, but his hands kept wandering.

'Stop that!' she half-screamed at him. But even as she voiced the wish, her mind told her it was not what she wanted. The towel had disappeared, and his steel arms were pressing her against his hard frame, her breasts crushed against his ribs, his hands wandering up and down her back, pressing her even closer. And every movement sent storm signals up her spine. 'Stop that,' she whispered against the tough skin over his heart, knowing that he couldn't hear, but protesting anyway, for the sake of her conscience. He pushed her slightly away, far enough so he could look down at her face, not so far that their hips broke contact.

'What's that?' he chuckled. 'You don't even know what you want, do you?'

'Of course I do,' she flared, her temper finally aroused. 'I want to be free of you, and to run—'

His hands dropped away from her, leaving her surprisingly chilled in the warmth of the night. She was trembling, uncontrollably shaking. 'So?' he laughed. 'Run away! You'll never have a better chance!'

She knew it to be true. Run away, her brain commanded. If you stay here you may never be free again. Run away! But her legs refused the order. She stood not more than two inches from him, with some of her muscles dragging her away, and others holding her still. She shook until her teeth chattered but not from the cold.

'You see,' he whispered softly, insidiously. 'You don't even know what you want. Relax. Let go. Do what you really want to do.'

Do what I really want to do? Here? All the years of her strict training were set immovably against what she really wanted to do! How could anything be so difficult to decide? Her trembling over-set her. She froze her muscles into rigid lines, stopped the tremors, and looked up at him. Do what you want to do! The silver moon, changing every colour to its own needs, seemed to have re-designed the world, changing it into a fairy wonderland completely removed from reality. Do what you want to do! She moved forward those tiny two inches, reached her hands up around his neck, and kissed him gently on one cheek. It was the first time in her life that she had ever instigated a kiss with an adult male. She giggled at herself, and as she laughed his head turned, and his lips were on hers, passively waiting. She took a deep breath, tilted her head slightly, and pressed against him with all her passionate strength.

As if waiting for that signal, his arms came around her again, holding her gently, hands roving from the curve of her hip up to the small of her back. Fire struck her down, breaking her concentration into small splinters, surrounding her with a shower of emotional meteorites, until he swept her up in his arms and carried her over to the soft grass at the poolside.

He laid her down gently in the welcome arms of the grass, and then dropped down beside her. His face shadowed hers, blocking out the moonlight, leaving her face in welcome darkness. He shifted his head as he trailed a line of kisses down her chin, her throat, and finally at the quivering peak of her breast.

And only then did sanity regain control. 'No!' she whispered, and then louder, 'No!'

He drew back slightly, trying to search out her face, but the shadows saved her. 'It's what you want,' he reminded her.

'No!' she replied, more strongly than before. 'Let me go!'

His head lowered towards her mouth again, but she intercepted it with both hands pressed between her lips and his. 'No,' she repeated, 'I—I'm not—'

'But it is what you want,' he insisted. She could see the gleam of his teeth as he smiled down at her.

'I—perhaps,' she confessed honestly, 'but I can't. Not without love. I just can't.'

'Chicken,' he laughed, drawing back from her. Somehow she managed to squirm out from under him, sitting up in the grass, using her hands to cover her breasts.

'Laugh if you want to,' she said bitterly. 'I didn't ask

for any of this. I—what kind of a man are you, Harry King? You spend the whole weekend in Atlanta with Eloise, and then you come back here and molest me.'

'Ah, that's it,' he chuckled. 'It's the "Eloise to Atlanta" bit that's upset you. A little jealousy going here?'

'No such thing!' she fired back at him. 'Althought how in the world you can expect me to—and what about Eloise?'

'What about Eloise?'

'Your aunt said that you—you and Eloise would—'

'Ah,' he chuckled. 'My aunt said!'

'Yes, and so did Eloise. So why don't you leave me alone and go relieve your male drives with her!' Katie scrambled to her feet, poised like a fawn, ready to break and run, if only she could know in which direction safety lay. He got up with her, standing with hands on hips, whistling.

'Well, aren't you going to say anything?' she demanded.

'Of course I'll say something,' he returned, with that monstrous grin on his face. 'The weekend was a great success. I have finally managed to solve Eloise's problem. She's staying over in Atlanta to buy her trousseau. I've given her a big cheque, and she'll be along on Tuesday or Wednesday for our little local celebration. Aren't you happy for her?'

'Yes,' she whispered, knowing that her heart denied it, knowing that the fairy garden had just turned into a deep, dark chilling cavern. Knowing that, despite the brightness around her, the moon had fallen from the sky and had broken into a million dusty pieces. 'Yes,' she repeated, 'I hope that—that she—and—I hope—' The words were too much for her. She turned on one silvery heel and fled into the darkness towards the house, holding her tears in check until she was safely in her room, with the door closed. And then she cried silently for all her unrealisable dreams.

CHAPTER FIVE

AFTER putting behind her a weekend that left her feeling somewhat lower than a snake's belly, Katie made every effort to keep out of the way. On Monday her efforts were successful. After a breakfast of cereal and silence, he disappeared for the rest of the day.

'Gone inventing,' Aunt Grace commented. 'Down cellar.'

Katie sighed, and busied herself with Jon, the kitchen, and housekeeping chores, in that order. That night Harry was absent from the supper table, for which Katie gave another sigh of relief, until his aunt spoiled the world with another one-line comment. 'Gone down to Johnson City,' she commented. 'To pick up Eloise at the airport.'

Katie hurried Jon through his supper, then packed him off upstairs, locking their door behind her, and never once stirring outside for the rest of the night—not even when she heard the car return, and Harry call up the stairs for her.

I'm asleep, she told herself, diving under the covers to prove it to herself. Her doorknob rattled as she hid in the darkness, and then footsteps went away. Eventually she was able to sleep.

But on Tuesday her luck ran out. She had sent her negatives to Erwin to be processed, since colour was beyond her meagre equipment, and one of the films had been returned with a flicker of movement in its corner. She found Harry alone in the kitchen, and screwed up her courage to ask.

'Go back to the same place?' he repeated. 'Easy, Katie.'

'I wouldn't ask, except it's right in the middle of the

panorama,' she stammered. 'I hate to ask you—'

'Why don't we go right now,' he suggested. 'Aunt Grace could watch Jon for a couple of hours, and Eloise won't wake up until noontime, at the earliest.'

So once again they were in the Jeep, riding up the side of the mountain, and out on to the flat saddle where they had stopped before. Ten minutes of walking, with only two cameras to weigh her down, brought them to the edge of the cliff. Rather than take another chance, Katie set up the Hasselblatt and re-took the entire panorama. But there was something in the distance that intrigued her: a little notch in the opposite hills through which the Nolichucky River ran, on its way to join the French Broad, and eventually to become the Tennessee River.

'I want to get one more shot with the Minolta,' she called to him, 'but I can't quite get the angle.'

'How about up on this cairn of rock,' he suggested. She looked at the natural pile that stood out from the rest of the area, like a pillar from a ruined Greek temple.

'I don't think I could climb it,' she said hesitantly.

'It's not so bad,' he laughed. 'Watch.' He went around to the back. She could hear his hands and feet scrabble against the sides, and a grunt or two as he powered his way up, then there he was, some ten feet above her, calling down.

'Not too hard,' he yelled, 'but maybe you'd do better to let me take the picture for you. Tie the little camera on to this string.'

She reached up for the wavering end of the twine he was lowering. It would have to be the Minolta, of course, with the telescopic lens. She fastened the camera securely in its case, and tied and twine carefully around the carrying handle. 'Don't let it bounce against the side,' she yelled up at him.

He waved in acknowledgement, leaning out from the top so the line would fall straight and unencumbered. Katie, standing directly under him, could see it all happen, but was unable to do anything about it. One of the loose rocks under his foot slipped. He backed off from it to regain his balance, but the stone, some ten pounds of igneous rock, broke loose, bounced once or twice on its way down, struck hard at the base of the pillar, and bumped over the edge of the cliff and out of sight.

It all happened so quickly that Katie did not notice, until seconds later, that the rock had struck off her left foot. And then the pain came. Sharp, insistent, piercing. She screamed once, and then darkness closed in.

When she drifted back to consciousness she was in the back seat of the Jeep, with her leg propped up on a folded blanket. Harry had just collapsed on to the front seat when some small noise she made alerted him.

'Are you all right?' he asked anxiously.

'Yes,' she muttered between clenched lips. 'Give me a few minutes. It'll all go away, I'm sure.'

'Like hell it will,' he returned. 'As soon as I can catch my breath—I think I almost broke my back carrying you down here—we're headed for the hospital. You'll have to hang on. It's all the way over to Erwin.'

'I can make it,' she assured him, wondering if it were true. He drove like a madman, down the mountain, through Ernestville, slowing only when he crossed the corporate boundary of Erwin. Even there he was somewhat over the speed limit as he wheeled down Sinasta Drive, behind the Unicoi County Memorial Hospital, and squealed to a stop at the emergency entrance. He left her in the car while he dashed inside, but moments later was back with help, and a rolling stretcher.

'I'm not hurt that much,' she told them feebly. She really believed it. They didn't. Tender hands moved her on to the stretcher. All she saw of the hospital interior was a series of high green-painted ceilings. Several unseen hands touched her swollen foot. She heard a murmur of consultation, and then they wheeled her away from the bright lights of the emergency room into the relative darkness of the X-ray section. Much to her surprise Harry stayed by her side all the way, holding her hand. No one in authority made any objection.

An hour later the doctor was back at her side, a satisfied smile on his face. He gestured, and a nurse appeared on her other side with a hypodermic needle. Thoroughly cowed by officialdom, Katie presented her arm on command.

'A small problem,' the doctor told her. The smile he wore looked artificial, as if he were tired from a long list of other 'simple' problems. 'You have a cleft in your left metatarsal,' he beamed at her, 'and a considerable oedema.' She was already feeling the effects of the injection, and felt as if she were floating about two inches above the rubber mattress. Obviously he was congratulating her for some outstanding accomplishment.

'That's nice,' she muttered sleepily. 'Is it catching?'

'What he means is that you've got a broken foot,' Harry interpreted. 'Come on, Henry, put it into English.'

'Ah, yes,' the doctor replied. 'When are you going to come help with that problem I told you about with the CAT scanner?'

'Right after I get my girl back,' Harry snorted.

'Oh! *Your* girl. I didn't understand. Okay, here's what we have to do. The foot has to go into a cast, but before we can do that, we have to get the oedema down. The swelling,' he added hastily. 'So we have to admit her, and put her in ice-packs and things like that. Say a day, two days. Then we have to plaster the foot up. Takes about, oh, two, three weeks before she can walk—with a walking cast, that is. And maybe, oh, altogether, six weeks until everything is back to normal.'

'But I can't do that,' Katie wailed. 'I have to go to a wedding. Marion would kill me if I missed. I know she would. I have to go—' But her words were getting softer and softer, and eventually they faded away, as she did, into sleep. The two men standing over her beamed at each other.

'Nice-looking girl,' the doctor said. 'Nice.'

'Yeah, nice,' Harry returned softly, with a proud lilt in his voice.

It was four days later before he was allowed to come and take her away. Her foot was weighed down with a tight plaster cast that covered all except her bare toes, and went up her leg to just below the knee.

'Now don't forget,' the doctor commanded, 'lots of rest. Make no attempts to walk. Keep the foot elevated as much as possible. Don't get the cast wet. Take two of these pills at bedtime, and whenever you feel pain during the day. No more than six a day. Got it?'

'She's got it,' Harry assured him. 'She'll do just as she's told, believe me.'

'I will not,' Katie mumbled under her breath.

'What?' Harry bent over and stared at her. The gleam was back in his eyes again.

'I said yes,' she stated clearly. And then, under her breath again, 'Arrogant man!' But he was too busy with last-minute papers and instructions. Or at least he seemed to be.

A hospital attendant pushed her to the door in a wheelchair. The Mercedes was standing outside, in a no-parking zone. A friendly policeman was leaning on the hood. He straightened and waved a casual greeting to Harry before walking away. She could not hold back the little dig. 'You have a lot of friends in this town?'

'Not really,' he laughed. 'It's the name. The King family is well known in these parts. I never tell anybody that I don't come from the famous branch. Nobody seems to care, and I enjoy it. Any other witticisms you want to get off?'

Her eyes were big as she shook her head, and a tear moistened the corner of one eye. 'Oh come on,' he laughed, as he picked her up and transferred her to the back seat of the car. He sat her down sideways, her foot resting on the seat, then propped her up with a couple of foam-rubber cushions. 'Okay now?' She nodded her thanks and surreptitiously wiped her eye.

'Oh. One more thing,' he said. He squeezed into the back seat with her, smoothed back the hair from her forehead, and gently kissed her. 'I've wanted to do that for the longest time,' he laughed. 'Your knees didn't buckle this time?'

'No,' she said gravely, 'I think I've been inoculated against kissing.'

'Well, we'll have to see about that when you get better,' he replied.

They started for home. Strange to think of the mountain house that way, her mind told her. Home? The day was exceptionally bright. Two crows swooped down, doing acrobatics over the car, as they left town. 'That's my welcome committee,' Katie said gleefully.

'Of course,' he replied, and sounded as if he meant it. She tried to carry on the conversation in the same vein, enquiring after Jon, Aunt Grace, and—heaven forgive me, she thought—Eloise. But when they pulled up at a traffic light on the outskirts of Erwin he turned and looked at her. 'You know, I hate gabby women,' he said.

'O-oh!' Her voice started off normally, but rose to an injured squeak. They made the rest of the trip in silence. An infuriating man, she thought, concentrating on the scenery. An abominable man! And if I just had my car—and if I just had my car it wouldn't make the slightest bit of difference, because I wouldn't be able to drive it if I wanted to. And that's the end of that excuse. There's nothing left to keep me here, the argument with herself continued. And I want to go, don't I? And there it surfaced. No longer hiding in her subconscious, what she really wanted to do faced her. 'Of course you don't want to go, you little fool,' she muttered under her breath, 'even if he is the most despicable man on earth!'

Aunt Grace met them at the front gate, a troubled expression on her face. 'They had three different kinds of wheelchairs,' she offered apologetically. 'I didn't know which one to choose, so I had them send all three. Is that all right, Harry?'

'Of course it is,' he told her. He opened the car door, meaning to pick Katie up, but she waved him away. She shifted herself along the seat until both feet were out of the door. But the minute she started to elevate herself he put an end to it by swinging her up in his arms and depositing her in the blue and silver wheelchair. 'I could have hobbled that far,' she protested.

'No, you couldn't,' he assured her. 'Henry said no walking at all. That means not even an attempt. For three weeks. Now look here. This chair is battery-operated. And the control is right here.'

Her sense of rebellion faded as Aunt Grace came over to kiss her, fussing around her as if she were the reigning queen. 'We missed you,' the older woman told her. 'Jon took it all very badly, and the rest of us agreed with him.'

'Where is Jon?' she asked.

'Napping. We've had to re-arrange the house, you know. Well, of course you don't know. You'll see.' She leaned over the chair again, her mouth close to Katie's ear. 'Make him show you his arms,' she whispered. 'A perfect cure!'

'Come on,' Harry called, 'let's get this show on the road, girl. Show us how well you can operate that thing.'

It proved to be no trouble at all. A toggle stick which could be swerved in any direction controlled both direction and speed. After a preliminary miscue or two, she started off across the bridge and up to the front door, where she met her first surprise. The four steps up from the ground had been removed and replaced by a cement ramp.

'I think it's dry enough,' Harry said. 'They didn't get it finished until midnight last night.'

She guided the chair up the ramp and into the hall. 'But how do I get upstairs?' she enquired.

'You don't,' he said. 'Straight down the hall to the dining room.'

She drove down the hall and turned into the familiar dining room, only to find it not familar at all! 'We converted it into a bedroom for you,' he said. 'I hope you don't mind. We had to use the dining room because its next to the kitchen, and there's a bathroom adjacent to it.'

'But you shouldn't have done all this! I—may I speak to you alone, Harry?' Aunt Grace took the hint and vanished. Katie swung her chair around to face him.

'All of this,' she said slowly. 'The chair, the room, the hospital—it's all too much to ask. After all, I imposed myself on you by sheer coincidence. I don't want to put you to such trouble. I think I had better go home.' She sounded wistful, and could not help it.

He walked over to the floor-to-ceiling window and brushed the heavy curtain to one side. Without turning round he said, 'I was afraid you'd feel that way. I found your home telephone number in your bag, and called your mother. We had a long talk—and then she had a longer talk with Aunt Grace, from which I was excluded. The result is, your mother wants you to stay. Your grandmother wants you to stay. Aunt Grace wants you to stay. And I want you to stay. After all, you wouldn't be in this fix if it hadn't been for my carelessness. And you can see it will be no trouble for us. I hired young Mary Sutmore from down by Tilson's Mill way, to come in and do for us all.' He paused for a moment, still staring out the window. 'At least think it over for a day or two?' He turned round to face her. She could see the look of intense concern on his face.

'You said—you want me to stay?' He nodded his head. 'Well, I—I think—all right. At least, I'll think it over. But I do have to go soon. Marion's wedding is in—'

'Three weeks,' he said solemnly. 'Not much time, but we'll make do.' The phrase rattled around in her tired head. We'll make do? We'll make do what? But the trip had been too much for her, and she dared not put the question.

The laughter had come back into his voice. 'And now we'd better get you out of that chair and into bed. You need to have your foot up in the air.' Without waiting for her to comment he lifted her up and deposited her on the bed. 'And now I'll help you into your nightgown.'

'The devil you will,' she said coldly. 'That's the quickest way I know to convince me I ought to leave for Ohio this minute, even if I have to walk.'

'Spoilsport,' he chuckled. 'I'll call in the Ladies Brigade and they'll get you into a nightgown. By the way, I put the rest of your leaves in the bureau drawer.'

'My leaves?'

'Those things you were so keen about picking up on the mountain.' And with that he disappeared round the half-opened door.

She laughed aloud, the first real mirth she had felt in four days. 'Now, if I could only cast a spell. What the devil was it that Grandmother used to say? Sorrel soothes, sassafras is for sighs, indigo for injuries— whatever the devil was that recipe for love potion?'

So when Aunt Grace and Mary Sutmore came in to get her undressed and settled, she was giggling away as if hospitals and broken feet were the order of days past. When Mary brought her supper on a large tray, she was accompanied by the master himself, and life seemed almost worth living.

Little Jon came with the dessert. That is to say, they arrived at the same time. The little boy stood beside the bed and stared at her as if she were a stranger. Then, struck by some memory, he struggled up on to the bed, yelled 'Birdie' at her, and jumped into her arms. His gurgle was infectious. Kate laughed back at him, tickled his ribs, and told off both set of toes with 'this little piggy' before Harry put a stop to it all, and had him carried off for a bath and bed.

'Well?' he asked her, when Mary and the baby had gone. 'Is this all satisfactory?' Katie looked around the room. She was in a marvellously comfortable double bed, set against the wall where the sideboard had formerly stood. A huge mahogany bureau, which must have broken four strong backs on the way in, took up the other wall. A desk, two deep chairs, a footstool, and a small scatter-rug made up the rest of the furnishings. It all seemed to huddle in corners of the vast room. 'I wanted to keep the floor clear so you could use your chair,' he added. 'The bathroom's through that door. We had to take the door off the bathroom so you could drive your chair through. I had them put a curtain up in its place.'

'Why—it's grand!' Katie assured him. 'I just can't believe that you've gone to all this trouble for me. Only—'

'Only what? Something about it bothers you?'

'Well, I hate to stay here and have Mary wait on me. There's something wrong with her foot, isn't there? She limps.'

'Yes,' he sighed. 'A congenital deformity. Don't worry your head. Mary can get along fine. And I have plans to get it taken care of. Off to sleep now.' He bent over the bed and dropped a kiss on her forehead. It was well-intended, she knew, but it still made her angry. That wasn't the sort of kiss she really wanted. But he was gone before she could marshal the words.

It was the infernal creaking that woke her up. Creak, snap, creak, snap, punctuated from time to time by a discreet cough. Katie forced one eye open, and immediately blinked it shut. The sun was shining in the window, low on the eastern side of the house. And someone was bending over her, leaving a trail of lavender scent in her nose. The creaking began again, with more enthusiasm. Warily she opened both eyes.

Her first impression had been correct. The sun was at the windows, and the creaking noise came from just off to her right. She turned her head slowly in that direction.

'Oh, my goodness,' Aunt Grace said with considerable satisfaction. 'Did my rocking chair wake you up? I knew it was noisy, but it's the only one available down here. I thought I would have a rock while I knitted, you know. Good morning.'

'Good morning.' Katie tried to smile, but it got tangled up with a yawn, and both lost out. 'No, your chair didn't wake me up,' she lied. 'I was waking up anyway. I hadn't noticed the rocking chair in here before.'

'No, it wasn't. I had Harry carry it about a half hour ago, and he dropped it. But that didn't wake you up, thank goodness. And then I thought I would sit and rock for a while, and I dropped my needles, and that didn't wake you up either. Thank goodness.' The second thanks were a little slow in coming, almost as if she were exasperated that the noise *hadn't* wakened her. 'So then I decided to knit some more.'

'Excuse me,' Katie interjected, 'but that seems to be a very strange piece of knitting. A scarf?'

'Of course not, my dear. It's a sleeve. I don't really knit any more. I made a sweater for Harry, but one of the sleeves turned out to be two feet long, and he said something very nasty. So I don't knit any more. I just work on this sleeve when I feel depressed. And pull it all apart when I feel better. Are you wide awake now?'

'I think so. Do you feel depressed today?'

'Of course I am. There's a problem. Otherwise why would I want to wake a guest up at eight o'clock in the morning?'

'That late? I'm—I'm stunned. Why are we whispering? Are we in a conspiracy of some kind?'

'Why, of course we are! That woman is still here! This is becoming a serious situation. We have to get busy!'

'Yes, I see that we do.' Katie noticed that a tear was forming in the corner of the older woman's eye. Whatever the problem was, it bothered her a great deal, and her sharply insistent tones were merely a cover-up for a very miserable old lady. 'Busy at what?' Katie asked.

'Are you not feeling well this morning, my dear? I

hope—this injury to your foot—you seem to be just the slightest bit dense this morning!'

'Ah—well—it must be the aftershock from my travels. It's reduced my—whatever. Perhaps you could explain again?'

'I can't do that. I haven't explained before, yet. I mean, this is the first time I've tried to explain. Now, listen carefully. Unless we do something quickly, Harry is likely to take it into his head to marry that—that person. And we can't allow that now, can we?'

'No, of course we can't allow that. Who?'

'Who? Eloise, of course. Whom did you think! We just can't allow that, can we?'

'No. Certainly not!' Here was a point where Katie felt in total agreement with the old lady. Total. 'So, therefore, we'll do—what?'

'There's only one foolproof way to keep him from marrying that woman. And that's for him to marry someone else instead!'

Katie sighed and wished she could get her mind untracked. Without a doubt Aunt Grace had the gem of an idea buried in all this conversation, and all it needed was a little careful mining to get it out. 'Yes, I can see that that would certainly solve the problem,' she agreed. 'Is there a bottle of aspirin on that table? I feel that I'm going to have a headache very soon.'

'In a minute, dear. We must get our plan settled before anyone else comes in.'

'Yes, of course. Plan?'

'What we need to do is arrange for you and Harry to be in close proximity for a while. Propinquity is the solution to our problem. After a few days of exposure he could hardly resist you, could he?'

'You mean Harry—him and me? You—must be kidding!'

'That's terrible English, dear. Of course, you and Harry. Who else? He has noticed you, hasn't he?'

'Noticed?' Katie squeaked. 'He does seem to have a

very low female resistance-level. He believes deeply in that song about loving the girl he's near. Any girl. But you must understand, Aunt Grace, that what he has in mind is definitely not marriage. Not with me, anyway.'

'You mean he's made some improper advances?' Aunt Grace mustered up a smile that could easily be called Cheshire Cat. 'Well, that just proves what I said—he's interested.'

'I know he's interested,' Katie said sombrely. 'But I don't think I'm interested in what he's interested in, if you follow?'

'Don't underestimate yourself,' the older woman returned. 'Nothing would suit me better than a wedding between Harry and yourself.'

'You make that sound as if I only need to—and—and what about Eloise? Doesn't she have anything to say? You think she's going to sit still while I snatch at her man? Or what about Harry? Doesn't he have anything to say?'

'As far as the Harrys of this world are concerned, my dear, the answer is no. I see that your education has been sadly neglected. Sex is an inherited trait, but marriage is an acquired taste, and the female of the species has always been the best teacher in that lovely subject. Now, what can you do that Harry would be interested in?'

'Me? Not much. All I seem to do is get in his way. I break a mean foot, of course.'

'Skilfully done, my dear. That was second on my list of suggestions. Not necessarily a foot, of course. Now he has to keep you at hand for a suitable period. Excellent.'

'Yes, I thought I did it rather neatly,' Katie returned wryly. 'But since I have only two feet there's little chance for a repeat performance. Outside of that I can cook, sew, keep house—'

'Nice for later. Worth nothing now. What else?'

'I really think Harry's only interest is in how well I might do in his bed. And I don't do that at all, frankly.'

'How nice. What else?'

'I—I take pictures. I'm really very good at it.'

'That might help, but not much. Every now and then Harry needs pictures of his experiments. But he calls in a professional from Johnson City. Anything else?'

'No, that's about—oh no. When I helped my father in the studio he always had trouble with the books. So when I went to college I majored in Business Administration. I never did anything with it, you see, but I did study.'

'Aha!' Aunt Grace pounced. 'You're a secretary— and with a college degree!'

'Well, not exactly. I studied all that, but all I ever got to do is sort the mail, and file things, and type out bills. Things like that.'

'Exactly what we need,' the old lady crowed. 'Exactly! You're a college-trained secretary!'

'Okay, okay,' Katie sighed in surrender. 'If you say it real fast, I suppose you're right. Yes, I'm a high-priced what you said.'

'And that's exactly what we need around here,' Aunt Grace returned. There was a smile of relief on her face, and she tapped her bottom lip with her knitting needles as if her mind were going into high gear. 'Yes, very nice indeed. Now all you have to do is be helpful—very helpful. From time to time I'll offer a few suggestions, but you can safely leave the rest of the programme in my hands, my dear. So nice.'

'And Eloise?'

'There are many strange things going on in this house,' the old lady said. 'Harry is a brash young man, and intensely loyal. George Bradford was his closest friend in the world. George was engaged to Eloise. He was killed in a racing accident at Le Mans. Before he died, he managed to get Harry to promise him something. I don't know what.'

'You think he means to marry her on a promise?'

'I don't know,' Aunt Grace said sadly. 'Harry is a man who plays his cards close to his chest. He hides himself behind a mask of brash impertinence, and only gives you a look at his real self when it suits him. But don't worry. We'll put a spoke in Eloise's wheel somehow or another.'

She got up from the rocking chair with some difficulty, and stuffed her knitting back into its basket. 'Time for your meal,' she said. 'You just rest yourself. Mary will bring it.' And then, looking thoughtfully down into the basket, 'I do believe I'll unravel this whole thing tonight and put it away.'

CHAPTER SIX

It was another three days later, a Friday, before Katie felt secure enough to venture out into the open. The fair weather still held, but there was a nip in the air. Harry and Eloise had disappeared shortly after lunch. Aunt Grace was off for her nap, and Katie played on the patio with Jon and Mary. The little boy had been smitten by the powered wheelchair. He sat in Katie's lap, urging her on at full speed, yelling at the top of his voice, 'Choo choo!'

'He must be mad about trains,' Katie laughed.

'You would be, too,' Mary told her, 'if you had an uncle like Harry King. Have you been down to the workshop yet? Trains everywhere. I've never seen anything like it in my life!'

'You mean model trains? I can see him at that! Does he have any other hobbies?'

'Everything, I think,' the younger girl replied. 'Amateur radio, trains, aeroplanes, photography, automobiles—everything.'

'Have you known him long, Mary?'

'All my life. My mother worked here for his mother, you know. I used to come up here every day during the week, until that ladyfriend of his put up a fuss. Doesn't bother me, of course. Mr Harry, he's been paying me regular, even though I didn't come. And now, in two weeks, comes the fun.'

'Two weeks? What happens then?'

'Oh, he wants his aunt to go to the World's Fair over at Knoxville, but she can't travel alone. So, she and I, we're going off to the Fair together. Mr Harry is arranging it all. We fly over from Johnson City, spend five days in a first-class hotel, and then Aunt Grace flies back.'

'You're not coming back with her, Mary?'

'Oh no. I'm going directly to Atlanta, for an operation on my foot. Mr Harry arranged that, too. He's a wonderful man. Just wonderful!'

Well! He's a wonderful man, Katie thought. Mary thinks so. Aunt Grace thinks so. Eloise thinks so! And what about me? Do I think so? 'I don't want to know,' she mumbled aloud.

'What?'

'I said what kind of a bird is that sitting on that bush?'

'That's a cardinal. There's a pair live around here regular. Is it true what Aunt Grace says, you got the powers?'

'No. That's pure superstition. There's no such a thing! How in the world can we ever get equal rights for women if we believe such stupid things?'

'But you did put a curse on Mr Harry—and cured his boils, too.' Katie looked carefully at the girl. No doubt about it. She wanted to believe! How do you convince someone like that that it's all mumbo-jumbo? 'I only made up a herb poultice,' she offered lamely.

'Katie! Katie Russel! I want to talk to you!' Harry came striding up the ramp from the cellar.

'I think he's mad. I'm gonna run,' Mary giggled. 'And I'll take the baby with me!'

'Coward!' Katie called after her.

'What's this I hear about you being a secretary?' Harry wasted no time in getting right to the point, and he *was* mad. She could almost see smoke coming out of his ears.

'I'm fine, thank you,' she said. 'How are your boils?'

'My boils?' He looked down at his arm, puzzled. 'I do believe that they're cured. Stop changing the subject.'

'What was it?'

'My aunt tells me that your new cover story is you are a college-trained secretary, who knows everything there is to know about running an office! I find it just as hard to believe as that one about you being a professional photographer. Is it true?'

'It might be. But why should that make you so mad?'

'It might be true? Don't you think I've been watching the pair of you like a hawk? You almost had me believing that photography story—and now there's a sudden switch. Well?'

'All right, it's true,' she lied. After all, why should he have it all his way all the time? 'Would you like to see my college degree? It's in Business Administration.'

'There's a catch here someplace,' he snarled, 'and I'll find out what it is sooner or later.'

'Pooh, pooh,' she said airily, waving off his objections. 'And I hope I find you well too?'

'Stop playing games,' he said. 'Put up or shut up. Come on.' He started to walk away, heading straight for the cellar ramp. Katie sat where she was, half-smiling. He stopped as soon as he realised she was not moving. 'Well, are you coming?' he growled.

'I don't think so,' she said primly. 'Is there any reason why I should?'

'Oh, come off it. You know the second act in this play. I say, "Are you truly a marvellous office worker?" And you say, "Yes, of course I am." And I say, "Oh, how wonderful. I am all mixed up in paperwork, and you have been sent by heaven to help me." And then you say, "Of course I'll help you, Harry." And then we go down into my office and the plot unrolls!'

'What a wonderful script,' Katie said, with just a slight touch of disdain in her voice. 'Do you write all your own material, or do you have help?'

He stood with his mouth open, staring at her. 'You mean you're going to offer to help me?'

'Help you what? I haven't heard anything yet that would make me be inclined to help you with anything. How is Eloise?'

'To hell with Eloise,' he snarled.

'My sentiments exactly,' she retorted. 'My, you have a fine command of words.'

'Katie Russel, sometimes you make me so—' He turned so that she could only see his back. His hands were clenching and unclenching at his sides, and he was muttering under his breath. And then he turned round again.

'Hello, Katie,' he said calmly. 'How's your foot? Are you enjoying the air out here?'

'Okay,' she replied. 'Now I'll help you. You do need help, don't you?'

'Lord, yes,' he groaned. 'I've got papers piled up two miles high. Do you really know about that sort of thing? You will help?'

'I said it. I always keep my word.'

'Katie, that's wonderful—I think. C'mon.' This time she followed him, guiding her chair carefully down the ramp, through a pair of double doors, and into an air-conditioned workshop. It stretched almost the entire length of the house. Just as Mary had said, tables along the walls were filled with operating model trains, both steam and diesel. They were all busily going somewhere, between carefully modelled towns and mills and deserts.

'I wish I were a boy,' Katie marvelled. 'What a beautiful set of toys.'

'Now you're being insulting,' he complained. 'Those are definitely not toys. You are looking at an HO gauge model railroad. Everything is built to scale, and copied from real equipment. I've got one hundred and fifty model-miles of track there.'

'And you're playing with them?'

'Not a bit,' he laughed. 'Well, not at this moment. My computer is running them. We're testing this little thing.' He held up a little black box with an antenna on it. 'Most trains are controlled by running signals along the tracks,' he explained. 'In our case, every one of those engines is separately controlled by radio.'

'That's nice, but not new,' she lectured him. 'My brothers fly radio-controlled aeroplanes all the time!'

'Yes, but . . .' he said, 'but I can run each engine from this little box—sixteen of them at the same time—and each engine sends back information about where it is and what's around it. Oh, and on a clear day I can take this little box sixty miles away and continue to control them.'

'Complicated,' she snapped, 'but still a toy.'

'You think so, do you? Suppose we put this same control in a low-level missile and went hunting enemy ships?'

'You mean . . .'

'I mean, my dear little girl, that you shouldn't take everything you see at face value around here. This is part of a contract I'm working on for the Defense Department. And in the meantime it helps me with my trains. Which I do play with from time to time! Come on, the office is over here.'

She followed him again, shaking her head. Keep your mouth shut, she told herself. It will get sore if you keep jamming your foot in it. Don't take everything you see at face value around here. Especially not him. Lord, I wish I could understand him. I need to talk to Grandmother about this man. Or somebody who knows a little more about men than I do. And that person shouldn't be hard to find—except around this loony bin!

He pulled open the door to a glass-walled cubicle, snapped on a light, and stepped out of her way. Directly in front of her was an eight-foot table, serving as a desk. Papers were stacked helter-skelter across it in depths of up to a foot in some places. Across the top of everything was a faint film of dust.

'And that,' he sighed, 'is my problem. When you need me, call.' He started back out of the door.

'Hey, wait a minute,' she yelled after him. 'I don't have the slightest idea what's in this—or what to do about it.'

'Neither do I,' he yelled back at her. 'Let me know when you think of something.'

She spent the next five minutes repeating out loud all the words her father had promised would get her mouth washed out with soap. Then she spent another fifteen minutes searching for a duster and, finally, a full hour re-arranging the dust within the office. She was still mumbling to herself as she inspected the practically new IBM typewriter, the desk calculator, the data terminal, and the curious object that turned out to be a copying machine. She was still grumbling when Mary came down to call her to supper.

There were only three adults at the supper table. 'It's Friday night,' Aunt Grace explained. 'Harry and Eloise have flown down to Atlanta. They usually do, you know.'

The soup was excellent. Katie spooned it up without enthusiasm, trying to keep the others from discovering that it tasted like dishwater. The fried chicken was for finger-eating. Aunt Grace managed three pieces. Mary did away with four. Katie barely managed to swallow two bites from the tiny leg before her. Her mind was back on the roller-coaster. He's gone to Atlanta. With Eloise. Purely platonic, of course. Huh! You're better off without him, Katie Russel. Sure you are. Say it over a hundred times, *he means nothing to me*. Keep repeating it. They go to Atlanta almost every weekend. No wonder he's not the marrying kind. Why buy a cow when milk is so cheap! Damn!

Making a conscious effort to hide her emotions, she teased Jon as she spoon-fed him his mushed vegetables and his pears. Even the baby was being uncooperative, and by the time dessert came round a dismal silence reigned at the table. Kate pushed her dish away, and realised that her foot was aching.

'I'll give Jon a wash in my bathroom,' she announced.

'No need to bother,' Aunt Grace said. 'You look worn out, my dear. Mary will take care of Jon. You just crawl into bed and rest. After all, this is your first week out of the hospital, and you've worked hard all day!'

'If I did I don't know it,' she said soberly. 'But I am tired. Are you sure you can handle the baby, Mary?'

'I'm sure. You go motor along to bed. Mr Harry rigged up a non-skid stool in your shower, and left something to cover your cast. Try it out. I'll be in yelling distance in case you slip.'

Despite the fact that she felt dirty all over, Katie took one look at the shower arrangements and decided to make do with a sponge bath instead. It took twenty minutes to undress and crawl into bed. The moment her eyes closed something else flashed in front of her eyes, bringing with it a massive headache. What else had he said a week ago? He had finally settled Eloise's problem, and given her a large cheque to buy her trousseau with? Oh Lord, she sighed. In the middle of all my daydreams I had forgotten. The auction is over, the bidding is closed, and Harry King belongs to somebody else. Lock, stock, and barrel. So what's the damned use! I'll stay just long enough to get his paperwork in order, and then I'll split. Marion's wedding is just over two weeks away. I'll be there. Damn the man!

Sunday was no better. Aunt Grace and Mary went off to church, with Jon in attendance. Katie wheeled herself down to the office again, and dived into the mass of papers. She scarcely came up for air until Wednesday noon, when Aunt Grace tracked her down.

'This won't do at all,' the older woman said sternly. 'The plan was to get Harry and yourself together. Instead, you're locked up down here and he's off every day with Eloise.'

'It's not my fault,' Katie mumbled. 'He knows all about our so-called plot, you know. He needs help down here, but can't you see he's laughing at us? We're too late. Did you know that Eloise was shopping for her trousseau—on Harry's money?'

'Sour grapes,' Aunt Grace responded. 'There's many a slip 'twixt cup and lip. And like that. His boils are all cured. Did you know that? Your potion was pretty good.'

'It didn't even inspire a thank you from him,' Katie answered mournfully. 'I think I'll quit. Or commit suicide, or something. Do you think that might teach him a lesson? If I jumped out my bedroom window and lay dead at his feet?'

'I hardly think so,' the aunt said a little nervously. 'It's only two feet down from the bottom of your window to the ground. I wish—'

'Aha!' The voice from the door was filled with laughter, and perhaps just a touch of triumph. 'I've caught you both at it, have I? Having a council of war?'

'Oh my! You startled me, Harry,' his aunt returned. 'I've told you hundreds of times that you—'

'Thousands of times!' He strolled over to the table to examine Katie's progress. What had been total disorder had now been reduced to three separate piles of papers, stacked with some neatness.

'I just remembered an errand,' Aunt Grace said, and made for the door.

'I'll bet you did,' Harry responded. 'Going to consult your occult books?' The words sounded cruel, but the look of affection that he gave her smoothed the path. Katie was startled by the thought. This big, brilliant man loved and respected his aunt totally. And they understood each other!

'I wish I did,' Katie mumbled under her breath.

'You wish you did what?' He walked over and sat himself down on the cleared corner of the table.

'I wish I had remembered an errand I had to do,' she replied nervously. What I really wish is that he would stop bothering me, she told herself. All he has to do is stand there and it bothers me. Why? It's obvious that all his intentions are bad. Why do I bother?

'What I wish,' he said, 'is that you would stop

squirming around so I could kiss you.' He took the two necessary steps to bring him over to her, and knelt down beside her chair. One of his arms slipped between her chair and her back, and squeezed gently on her shoulder. She watched, hypnotised, as his head filled up all her view, and his tender lips gently caressed hers.

It isn't fair, she screamed at herself. He has all the advantages. He's a domineering, arrogant—whatever. And he belongs to Eloise, you fool! The thought was enough to goad her into action. She stiffened in his arms, brought both her hands up in front of her and pushed against his strength. It had little effect. She turned her head, desperately trying to evade his questing mouth— and somehow the message got through to him. He slacked off his grip, backed an inch or two away from her, and studied her face.

'Catching cold?' he asked, amused at her futile struggles. 'Don't tell me you weren't joking about the inoculations?'

'Let me loose,' she snapped back at him. 'I told you before. I know what you want, and I don't want any of it. I'm not that kind of girl.' No, I'm not, she re-assured herself. He's passing the time of day with me. Eloise must have given him an hour off the leash. There's a big sign right between his eyes. It says, 'Taken!'

'Ah, we do have a problem.' He sighed, but it was too exaggerated to be real. 'In that case, let's get down to business.'

She caught herself staring at him, and forced her eyes to break contact. How about that! Switching from sex to business as if nothing had happened. How can he do this to me? She clenched her lips, and drove her chair back to the table. He came around behind her, and stood disturbingly close, with one hand on her shoulder. She could not resist a glance at those long tactile fingers.

'This pile is the easiest.' She pulled the first and smallest stack over in front of him. 'These people are paying you for past services. There's a total of—' She turned to consult the calculator, '—fourteen thousand, six hundred and fifty dollars in cheques among them all.'

He chuckled as he picked up the pile and leafed through it. 'I knew we were short of money somehow. Send all the cheques to the bank. Eloise will be happy to take them in. The deposit slips are in the file cabinet behind you. Then send a note to each of these people. Say "Thank you".'

'Nothing else?'

'Nothing else. Just "Thank you".'

She shrugged her shoulders and turned to look at him. He was smiling broadly, almost grinning. 'This next pile is social.' She handed him the biggest of the remaining piles. 'It includes twenty-two invitations to dances, sixteen invitations to speak at universities, and one invitation to the Governor's Ball.'

'The Governor's Ball. You might enjoy that, Katie.'

'I doubt it,' she gloomed. 'If this calendar is right, it was last Wednesday.'

'Ah. A tinge of sarcasm going there, have we?'

'What should I do with them all?'

'This.' He took the entire stack from her and dropped it into the capacious wastepaper basket under the table. 'Those who really mean it will write again. Next?'

'This last stack—' she stopped in mid-sentence. 'Why did you try to kiss me, Harry?' She tilted her head up to watch his eyes.

'Why? Well, let me see. I could say because you're the only lovely female within reach. Or perhaps I just like to kiss you. Or would you rather hear me say that I love you, Katie?'

She snapped her head round, away from the strange look in his eyes. 'I could believe the first one, even if I'm not lovely,' she said bitterly. 'The other two are impossible. I think you do it because you know it disconcerts me. And I know you don't love me. You're engaged to Eloise!'

'That's what she says,' he retorted. 'Who would you rather believe?'

'I don't know what to believe!' She banged her fists impotently on the arms of the wheel-chair, staring straight ahead to avoid looking at him. 'I don't know what to believe,' she repeated in a half-whisper. Both his hands came to rest on her shoulders. They moved inward, so his thumbs could gently massage her neck. The gradual comforting circlings relaxed her, released her tense muscles, so that she slumped down in the chair with a sigh.

'Some day soon I'll tell you,' he said in his deepest bass voice. 'I have promises to keep, and there are other people involved. When it's all settled, I'll tell you which one to believe. In the meantime, why don't you accept the idea that perhaps all three are true?'

'Oh, dear God,' she moaned, covering her face with her hands. But before she could think of a way to continue the conversation he had picked up the remaining stack of papers and was leafing through them.

'All these require answers,' he commented. 'Are you ready?'

She picked up a notepad, flexed her fingers, and nodded.

In a little under an hour they had completed the lot. In each case he gave her the name and address of the correspondent, scanned the letter in his hand, told her to write either 'Yes' or 'No' to each one, and dropped it on to the table.

'That's all?' she queried again. 'Just "No"?'

'Well, maybe you could put that in capital letters,' he offered, 'but I don't want to get too wordy.'

'Should I make copies?'

'Of the ones that get a "Yes", I suppose. There's a machine around here somewhere. With the "No's" forget it. Chuck them in the wastebasket. Any questions?'

She looked up at him with a dazed expression. 'Do I dare?' she squeaked.

'That's better. You'll make me a fine secretary, even if you are a crazy mixed-up kid.' He patted her shoulder and walked out the door. His hands were in his pockets, and he was whistling an old tune, something about 'The Girls He Left Behind Him!'

At four o'clock, still not finished, her foot told her she had had enough. She re-shuffled the papers on the table, covered the machines, and drove herself up the ramp and out on to the patio, looking for a quiet place to hide. She found it in a clump of rhododendron bushes just beyond the swimming pool. She manoeuvred herself into its shadow, clumsily elevated the foot rest attached to the chair, and leaned back, watching the flights of sparrows criss-crossing in the sky. A noise from the pool area attracted her attention. Eloise was walking slowly around the perimeter of the enclosure. When she saw Katie, she turned in that direction.

'Well, here's where you are,' the woman stated cheerfully as she came up to the wheel-chair. 'You've been buried in that office all day. That's a terrible imposition on an invalid. Can I get you something to drink?'

Katie was so startled that she was speechless for a moment. Eloise was obviously in the best of humours. Had she and Harry—? Too weary to reason, she nodded her head. 'It's a little chilly. A mug of coffee would be nice. Cream, no sugar.'

'Right away,' the smaller woman responded, and started for the kitchen. Katie watched her with a tinge of envy. Eloise walked with a wild hip-roll that was better than the death-dance of the Black Widow spider, and at every step she jiggled! And that's what the red-blooded American boys like, Katie sighed. And now, if Eloise turns into 'Miss Nice', what the devil am I going to do? You can't hate somebody who's got it all, just because she's got it, can you? You're darn well right you can, she told herself fiercely. Of course you can. What has she got that I haven't? Well mainly, she's got Harry. And I want him. It sounded so good that she said it out loud, 'I want him.' A little voice in the back of her mind said, 'Why?'

'I'm darned if I know,' she yelled up at the sparrows. They acknowledged her statement with a brief dip in her direction. Think of something, she commanded herself. You cannot let Eloise become the good guy. Think of something!

The little blonde was on her jiggly way back from the kitchen with two steaming mugs in her hands. As she watched, Katie repeated her new mantra. 'I hate Eloise,' she whispered over and over again. 'I hate Eloise!'

'That wasn't too long, was it?' Eloise asked. She passed one of the mugs over, and settled herself in the grass at the front of the chair.

'No, that's just fine,' Katie acknowledged, sipping at the mug. There was sugar in the coffee, but she mustered a smile, and sipped again.

'It's good to be able to come back here and relax,' Eloise continued. 'You've got no idea how tough it is down in Atlanta. Hot! Those TV lights are enough to burn you up. It's just too much.'

'It sounds like a very hard line of work,' Katie offered tentatively.

'You have no idea. You work and slave and posture for hours, all for a five-minute picture. In fact, a two-minute shot this last week. A TV commercial, you know. But the pay's good.'

'I couldn't imagine turning on the television and seeing myself,' Katie contributed. 'How do you get used to it?'

'Well really, after the first few months, it becomes no problem. It must seem glamorous to you, after working in some grubby office.'

'It's glamorous all right,' Katie chuckled, 'but I don't know about working in some grubby office. Most of my regular work is done outdoors.'

'Outdoors? But I'm sure Harry said you were some sort of office worker! Now why would he—'

'Perhaps he was teasing?'

'No, never that,' Eloise said. Her eyes were half-closed, reflective. 'That man never says a word that he hasn't thought out very carefully. Our Harry just never talks impulsively. Never. Except of course, when we went up to Atlanta.'

Brace yourself, Katie told herself. Here's where we come to the meat of all this goody-goody business. 'Did you enjoy your weekend?' she asked.

'Oh, it was the most,' Eloise gushed. 'We stayed at the Sheraton, of course. Saturday afternoon we went shopping. Dresses, unmentionables, the works. Harry is very meticulous. He insisted on staying with me all day, helping to choose, paying the bills. As you'll find out some day, Katie, a woman needs a whole new wardrobe when she's about to take a big step like this. And then we dined and danced into the wee hours. Harry, and an old friend of his. A rich old friend, I might say. All wonderful. You know, Harry has friends in all sorts of places. Maybe he could find somebody for you, dear. Would you like me to ask him?'

'N-no,' Katie managed to stutter. 'I wouldn't be interested in any of Harry's friends. 'So—you're finally going to take the big plunge? How soon?'

'Of course it's still a secret, you understand. But very soon. Within the next three weeks, my dear. I'm so excited!'

'Yes, of course you are.' Katie could feel an ache in that empty spot in the pit of her stomach. 'That's why Harry was so happy this afternoon?'

'Oh? Did you see him this afternoon?' The blue eyes glared at her suspiciously.

'In the office, for only a few minutes,' Katie explained. 'He looked at some of the mail, and dictated answers to several enquiries.' And tried to kiss me again. And ruined me for the rest of my life! How in the world can I settle down, look at some other man, after Harry?

'And I almost forgot to show you!' Eloise exclaimed, holding out her left hand. And there it is, Katie snarled at herself. The true brand of possession. A magnificent square-cut diamond blinked back at her from Eloise's third finger.

'It—it's very beautiful,' Katie stammered. 'Very—beautiful. But—I—would you excuse me, Eloise? My foot is aching. I've got to go get some more pills.' Without waiting for an acknowledgement she shifted the wheel-chair into 'drive' and started back towards the house.

'Of course,' the blonde called after her. She was making no effort now to hide the derision in her voice. 'Take something for it quickly. If you're sure it's your foot that's aching!'

CHAPTER SEVEN

SHE drove her chair across the patio at full speed, meaning to scuttle into the refuge of her room. The baby intercepted her. Jon was sitting on the floor of the kitchen, surrounded by acres of little toys, but all alone. As her chair clattered against the screen door his face lit up. 'Choo, choo,' he yelled, levering himself up to his feet. Katie braked the chair to a stop and held out her arms. The boy rambled across the floor with a huge grin on his face, and climbed up on the foot rest of the chair. She swept him up in her arms, forgetting her clash with Eloise in the sunshine of the child's smile. 'Choo choo,' the boy repeated urgently.

'Okay, choo, choo,' she returned solemnly. He squirmed around in her lap so he could see straight ahead, then waited, but not too patiently. When she still did not start the chair rolling he turned his little blond head and said demandingly, 'Choo, choo!'

'All right, already.' She laughed at him, and started the chair off at slow speed across the kitchen. They butted into the swing doors, and out into the hall. The boy began to bounce on her lap. She increased speed, and they zoomed up and down the length of the hall at full throttle, the child screaming in delight. On their fourth turn they barely missed running over Harry's foot as he came up the inside entrance to the basement.

'Hey,' he yelled.

'Choo, choo!' his nephew responded.

'Choo, choo, my foot!' he yelled, holding out his hand. 'You tell the engineer of that train to watch where she's driving.'

Katie brought the chair to a gradual halt, much to Jon's disgust.

'Now that's better,' Harry chuckled, as he came abreast of them. One of his hands dropped on to her shoulder. She flinched away from it. He looked down at her with a puzzled expression on his face, and stretched out his hand again. She backed the chair slightly, causing him to miss his target. He pulled back his hand and held it up before his eyes.

'No frostbite,' he observed, 'but it's distinctly cold around here. What's the problem, Katie?'

'I don't have a problem, Mr King,' she said.

'Brrrrr,' he retorted. 'Either the temperature is dropping fast, or you're really an Eskimo.'

'Are you finished criticising, Mr King?' she asked coldly. 'Jon and I were playing, and we would like to continue.'

'And I would like to talk seriously to you. Put the kid down.'

'You and I have nothing to talk about, Mr King.' She hugged the baby closer to her. Jon squirmed. 'Choo, choo,' he pleaded.

'You and I have a million things to talk about,' he repeated. 'Put the child down and come to the kitchen with me.'

'I have no intention of leaving Jon all by himself. Somebody else has already done that today. Please go away.'

'Damn it,' he roared. 'Eloise was supposed to be watching the baby. Where is she?'

'I'm sure I don't know, Mr King. Isn't it up to you to keep track of her?'

'Why the devil should I—oh, no you don't, girl. You don't get me off the subject that easily. Now, what's biting you?'

'Nothing's biting me, Mr King. And nothing is going to bite me. As soon as this child is settled with its mother I intend to call home and have someone come and get me!'

'Oh brother,' he moaned, running one hand through

his thick hair. 'Look, Katie, if it's because I left you alone this afternoon, it was only because I had to go into town for a few clothes.'

'Of course, Mr King. I understand. Too bad you couldn't get them all in Atlanta when you were on your shopping expedition!'

His eyes narrowed. He shoved both hands deep into his pockets and cocked his head slightly to the right. 'Shopping expedition? he queried. 'Who told you about that?'

'Who do you think told me?' she said sweetly. 'Who do you think rushed right over to be sure I heard it all?'

'Eloise, damn it! Well, sure, I took her on a shopping expedition. You wouldn't expect me to let her go into something like this without a decent wardrobe of clothes, would you?'

'I—I don't expect anything of you, Mr King. It's called a trousseau. She was so pleased when she showed me her engagement ring!'

'Ah!' His eyes lit up, and that infectious smile reappeared. 'So she really came out in the open, did she! Wonderful! It's about time. Eloise is a great believer in never letting the right hand know what the left hand is doing. Did you congratulate her?'

She stared up at him, her mind a cauldron of confusion. Two of a kind. Each accusing the other of being close-mouthed. And evidently they were both right—about each other of course. They—they'll make a lovely pair. As dishonest a pair as ever you could want! 'Yes, I congratulated her. My mother trained us all to do the right thing, even when it hurts.' But her mother had never trained her to keep the bitterness out of her voice, or the anger from her eyes.

He put one of his massive feet up on the foot rest of the chair. If only I dared, Katie thought, I'd run him over. How would that look in the local paper? 'Famous Inventor Wheeled to Death?' The idea was so intriguing that she missed what he was saying.

'I—what was that?' she asked.

'I said you have to understand about Eloise,' he repeated. 'She's a kid who came up from nothing. Her father was a share-cropper in Georgia. Eloise has come up a long way. She lives in a cut-throat world. A little miscellaneous lying, cheating and stealing are considered normal. But now she finally has a chance at the brass ring. If only she would stop trying to grab every prize in town, she could be very happy.'

'Why not,' Katie said soberly. 'As you say, she's got the brass ring. I'm—I'm happy for both of you.' I'm also becoming the biggest liar in history, she told herself. It was a struggle to keep the tears from flowing. She cuddled the baby closer to her, hiding her face in the cool silk of his hair.

'Choo, choo?' Jon pleaded.

'Yes, choo, choo,' she choked. She pushed the chair control forward and they started to roll down the hall towards the front door.

'Hey, what the hell?' he called after her. One of his heavy hands struggled against the movement of the chair. 'Why would you congratulate me?'

'Because you're very lucky to get such a beautiful woman as your wife,' she half-shouted at him. She pushed the toggle control to full speed. The chair bucked against him, and then broke free.

'Hey, wait,' he called, taking two steps down the hall behind them. 'You've got this thing all—'

Whatever he had intended to say got lost in the confusion. The big front door swung open. A beautiful red-headed woman stood in the door, a woman whose face seemed a replica of Harry's, although softened with a radiant beauty. She was about Katie's height. There was a suitcase in either hand, which she dropped on the floor immediately.

'Mama!' Jon yelled. He struggled and squirmed against Katie's circling arm. She stopped the chair, and the little boy wiggled down, ran across the intervening space, and threw both hands around the neck of the kneeling woman.

The two of them jabbered at each other, seemingly in full communication, although none of the words sounded like English. Then the woman stood up, still holding the baby close, and walked over to the wheelchair. 'You must be Katie?' she asked, extending her one free hand. 'I talked to Harry on the telephone last night, and he mentioned your name—about five hundred times, I believe. I want to thank you for looking after my little hellion. I'm Amanda, Harry's sister.'

'Yes, I'm Katie,' she stammered. The hand that held hers was firm, long-fingered—like Harry's of course. The eyes were blue, the complexion light, with a sprinkle of freckles just across the nose. And such a very determined nose! 'It was no trouble,' she continued. 'Jon has been the one long-suffering prize in all this mess. He's a wonderful child, Amanda.'

'And I'm glad to see you too, Amanda,' her brother said from just behind Katie's shoulder. 'It's so nice of you to drop in for a moment to pick up your kid!'

'No sarcasm, Harry,' his sister responded. 'And that's just what we're doing.' She turned back to Katie to explain. 'My husband has had some bad news,' she said quietly. 'He expected to be sent up to Richmond, and instead they've given him his unconditional release.'

She turned back to Harry. 'We expect to stay one or two days, brother dear, and then we'll be on our way. Sometimes, I don't think you love me, Harry.'

'Oh I love *you*,' he contributed. 'It's that idiot husband of yours that I can't stand. Where is he now?'

'He's out struggling with the luggage,' Amanda reported. 'He'll be along in a minute. He's had one terrible blow to his pride. And just remember one thing. I happen to love that idiot.'

'Well, there's no accounting for taste,' her brother laughed. He stepped around the wheelchair, lifted his sister up off the floor, baby and all, and kissed the tip of her nose. 'Choo, choo,' Jon squealed, caught in the crush.

Katie watched them, as Harry swung his sister and the baby around in welcoming circles. It reminded her too much of home, where the circle of her siblings would close around her to shut out all hurt and pain. Just thinking of it brought a tear to her eye, but no one else noticed, so she let it flow free.

There was a banging noise at the door, and a tall man, burdened with four suitcases, stomped into the hall. 'Where do you want all this junk?' he asked in a hard, clear voice. Without waiting for an answer he dropped them all on the floor in a jumbled pile, and stepped forward. He was looking at his wife. It might have been the sharp hiss of Katie's shocked intake of air that caught his attention. He looked down at the chair, and a surprised look flashed across his square blond head. 'Katherine,' he exclaimed. 'What the hell are you doing here?'

'Eubie?' she questioned, hardly believing it. 'Eubie Fairfield?' It was too much. There had been too many surprises in the day, too many pains, too many aches. She pushed the throttle to full speed, whipped around, and raced down the hall to her bedroom, leaving the hall full of people to watch in stunned silence.

By the time she was in the room with the door shut behind her she could hear pursuing footsteps. She fumbled frantically for the lock, then realised how un-usual it would have been for a dining room door to have a lock. She could see the knob rattle as the door started to move inward towards her. Without giving it much thought she jammed on the forward control of the wheelchair and rammed its foot rest up against the door. The little electric motor under her seat wailed at the load, but the door was gradually forced closed.

'Katie,' Harry yelled from outside. 'Open this door. We have to talk.'

'I don't have a thing to say to you,' she yelled back at

him. 'Go talk to Eloise. Leave me alone!'

'By God I will,' he roared. She could hear him stomp down the hall yelling 'Eloise' at the top of his lungs. Katie kept the nose of her chair grinding into the door until she was sure he had gone, then she wheeled herself around, drove over to the bed, and managed to struggle up out of the chair. Tears were blinding her, confusing her, as she toppled over on to the bed. 'I don't know what I'm crying about,' she mumbled. Could it be Eubie? Or Harry? Or—just the pain and loneliness that had struck her out there in the hall, when she suddenly realised that, despite their differences, they were all a family. Excluding her. And very suddenly the hall had become cold, dark, rejective. Very suddenly she had become the outsider, a long way from home.

'So what do you do now, Katherine?' she asked herself. 'The baby has his mother back. Eloise has her man. Even Eubie is safe with his family—damn that man. Aunt Grace is going to the World's Fair. So is Mary. And I might just as well go home to Ohio.' Acknowledging defeat was half the problem. The rest should be easy. She rolled over on to her back, banging her damaged foot against one of the bedposts. The sharp pain helped to clear her mind. She snatched up the telephone, and started to dial Humbersville, Ohio.

There was something wrong. The telephone did not ring at the other end. Perplexed, she depressed the handswitch and waited for the dial tone. Nothing happened. She rattled the telephone and thumped its base. Still nothing. Cursing under her breath she jammed the handset back on the cradle and stared at it. Her lifeline to the outside world had been cut off. She pounded an exasperated fist on her cast, trying to think of some way to escape. Walking was definitely out. But what else was available?

She swung herself back into the wheelchair and went over to the window. The green lawn still sloped down to the edge of the bluff. The bridge stood waiting, a patient slave to movement. On the other side, in the parking lot, her own VW, the Reliant, and the Mercedes, as well as a beautiful Jaguar. Driving her own car, she knew, would be impossible. The cast could not possibly fit the clutch pedal. But the Mercedes had automatic drive! If she could find the right keys, it offered a chance to take her escape. And she need only go as far as the nearest airport. As for her clothes, handling two suitcases was beyond her. She would have to leave them all behind.

Driven by determination, she wheeled round for the door, and then had second thoughts. Running away again. Her only solution to a series of difficult problems. Leaving behind her all the unfinished business—and Harry! Maybe just this once she could muster enough strength to see a problem through? Just one time, so that in the long dark years ahead she could remember that at least she had tried?

A knock on the door interrupted her reverie and, before she could answer, Mary opened it and came in. The younger girl was flushed with excitement, her cheeks a glowing red. 'Do you want me to help you get ready for supper?' she gasped.

'I—what's all the excitement?'

'You didn't hear it? Mr Harry has been roaming around the house like a chicken with his head cut off. He cornered Eloise in the library, and they must have had a real donneybrook of a fight! Even with the door closed I could hear some of it. And your name appeared in the conversation several times, Katie.' She broke into giggles as she went over to straighten out the bed. 'And so Eloise is hiding in her room and says she won't eat with us tonight, and she wants a tray in her room, but Mr Harry, he said, "the hell she will!"'

'And Mr King?'

'He's still in the library. Boy is he tying one on. Straight Bourbon, right from the bottle. Wow! And that's only half of it!'

'What's the other half?'

'Well, you don't know, I suppose, but Miss Amanda, she's just like her brother. When she's mad, look out! Anyway, she and her husband went out on the patio—and you should have heard her dress him up one side and down the other! Lord love us, she chewed that man up and spit him out! And guess what, Katie?'

'All right, I give up. What?'

'Well, your name came up in that argument several times, too. And then Miss Amanda, she stormed off to her room and slammed the door!'

'I—I think maybe I'd better skip supper, Mary,' she said nervously. All her courage had gone down the drain. 'I've got the feeling that I'm not going to like the main course tonight.'

'Oh, you can't do that,' Mary wailed. 'I'm making barbecued spareribs, Tennessee style. You said it was your favourite. We have got tables set up on the patio and everything, like a home-grown picnic.'

Yeah, spareribs, she thought to herself. You know better. If you step out there tonight the main course is going to be barbecued Katie Russel. Served with an apple in her mouth!

'I—I think I would better stay in my room,' she started to say, but at that moment a gleeful Aunt Grace came waltzing into the room. 'You've done it, Katie,' she carolled. 'You've done it, you marvellous person!'

'Done what?' she asked in bewilderment.

'You've got them fighting! I knew it you just kept at it that you would get a wedge going between them. Smart girl! And by suppertime they'll be up to the boiling point again, and we'll just sit there and make hay while the sun shines!'

'I wish I knew what you were talking about,' Katie said sadly. 'There are so many confusing conversations going on around this house that I think only Jon and I are on the same frequency. Eloise is mad at me. Harry is mad at me. Amanda is mad at me, and I suspect Eubie is, too. I'm not coming to supper. I'm going to sit here in my room, or maybe soak my head, or maybe run away. Where are the keys to my car?'

'They're hanging on the rack by the back door, along with all the other car keys,' Mary answered. 'I've got to scoot. Don't you dare miss supper.'

'Of course she won't,' Aunt Grace chimed in. 'This promises to be the best supper we've had since last Fourth of July.'

'And I suppose you think I'm going to provide the fireworks display,' Katie grumbled to her disappearing back. Well, you've got another think coming, she sighed to herself. It's back to Plan One. When in doubt, run. And if I go very quickly, and keep terribly busy, maybe I won't notice the pain so much! She snatched up a light jacket from the closet, and piloted herself into the kitchen without meeting anyone. From the patio outside she could hear Mary and Aunt Grace, as they arranged the tables for the barbecue supper. The rest of the house was quiet.

It took but a moment for her to discover the keyboard hanging in a dark corner. She rescued her own keys and those of the Mercedes. Then she whirled her chair around and made for the front door.

It was a struggle to get the door open, because of its strong retaining spring, but eventually she managed to edge her way out on to the ramp. She closed the door softly behind her, and pointed the chair towards the bridge. The chair performed its little miracle silently. It spanned the bridge quickly, and delivered her to the door of the Mercedes. She fumbled with the keys, managed to open the door on the driver's side, and brought the wheelchair up parallel to the car.

The transfer from chair to car-seat was difficult. She was perspiring when she finally fell back into the soft cushions. Her foot had received two smart cracks against the side of the car, and the sudden pain had brought tears to her eyes. Sniffing them away, she struggled to swing her feet into the car. The weight of the cast on her left foot made it too cumbersome to handle easily. She stopped to catch her breath, and to run a finger through her unruly hair.

Using both hands to help, she finally manoéuvred the recalcitrant member into the car. She was out of breath, upset, and still sniffling from the pain. The lock evaded her trembling fingers. Not finding it, she dropped her head into the cradle of her arms across the steering wheel, and had a good cry.

'Turn off the waterfall,' she mumbled to herself a short time later. She pushed herself back into the seat and looked down to where her left foot was resting. It was edged into the corner, on top of the high-beam light button. She flexed her right foot between brake and accelerator a couple of times. In the wiggling struggle to get settled she had come all disarrayed, she noted. Three of the buttons on her blouse had come unbuttoned, and her skirt was rutched up underneath her almost to hip level. She shook her head in disgust, flexed her right foot again, and bent over to look for the ignition lock. Her hand wavered towards it, but the key missed the hole twice.

'It's a little further to the right,' the voice at her ear said softly. She was so startled that she dropped the keys to the floor, and no amount of stretching and struggling would bring them to hand again. She gave it up, disgusted, and looked up over her shoulder.

'And just where do you think you're going?' Harry King, at his sarcastic best!

'I—It's none of your business,' she spluttered. 'I—I'm going home. I called my mother and she said I should come home.'

'Among other things, you're a little liar, Katie Russel,' he said. 'The telephone's been out of service since early this morning.'

'Well, if I *had* talked to her she would have told me to come home,' Katie said woodenly. 'A—and I'm going!'

'So there!' he added. 'But not in my car, girl. That

would be grand larceny. They treat car-thieves pretty
badly around these parts, you know.'

'I wasn't trying to steal your damned car,' she told
him bitterly. 'I was only—borrowing it. That's all.
Borrowing it.'

'Lost your cool, Katie? Running away?' He opened
the car door to its widest, and slipped a hand under her
knees.

'What are you doing!'

'Well, right now I'm looking,' he replied. 'Lord, what
lovely legs you have!'

'Don't you dare touch me,' she hissed. 'Don't you
dare!'

'No. Of course not.' But he obviously didn't mean
it. He swung her up in her arms, careful not to bang
the damaged foot, and carried her back to the wheelchair. 'We can't have much more of this,' he continued. 'You're not the lightest girl in the world, you
know.'

'If you would leave me alone,' she snarled at him, 'you
wouldn't have this terrible trouble. I hope you slip a disc,
or—or get a hernia, or something.'

'All right, that's enough!' There was a warning note in
his voice that she took trembling notice of. She pursed
her lips to block off any further words, and took a
stranglehold on the arms of the chair.

'And now, Miss Russel,' he continued softly, 'we're
all waiting for you at the supper table. Giddyap. Hi Ho,
Silver!'

'Don't be a wise guy,' she snapped, through clenched
teeth. But she complied, nevertheless, driving the chair
slowly back across the bridge. He sauntered behind her,
stopping at the far side of the walkway.

'What are you doing?' He was swinging the wire-mesh
gate closed behind them. He snapped the padlock, and
patted it.

'Just making sure,' he chuckled. 'I'm not much for the
forty-yard dash. I don't think I could do it again tonight.

In fact, if I hadn't seen you from the library window you would have been long gone, wouldn't you?'

'You can't keep me here if I don't want to stay,' she told him coldly. 'Is that what I am? A prisoner?'

'No,' he snapped back. 'You're my honoured guest, and I told your mother I would take care of you. Now drive that damned thing round the house. We're going to have supper if I have to spoonfeed you all the way.'

She could see the glare in his eyes, the twitch of muscle at the corner of his mouth, and the clenched fist that he was slamming into his other palm. 'You wish that could be, me,' she retorted, and set her chair in motion at full speed, trying to put some distance between them.

She did, in fact, beat him to the table, but only just. Everyone else was there waiting. Even Eloise had decided to come down. Mary had arranged four folding card-tables in a row, covered them with a single white tablecloth, and set out paper plates and plastic utensils to make a banquet table for the night. A series of bug-killer lights hung around the perimeter of the patio. All of them were carrying on a desultory conversation when Katie wheeled round the corner, and then silence reigned.

Aunt Grace signalled her to the far end of the table. 'There's more room up here,' she said.

'I'm sorry to be late,' she murmured. Nobody else besides Aunt Grace looked as if they felt any particular interest in the whole affair. Then Harry pulled out his chair at the opposite end of the table, and the conversation began again.

'These spareribs are marvellous,' Katie exclaimed, trying to lift herself out of the doldrums.

'It's all in the marinade,' Mary acknowledged. 'You remind me sometime and I'll get you the recipe. It's Mr Harry's favourite food. With turnip greens and okra.'

Katie watched while Aunt Grace dissected the ribs with a dainty movement of her knife, and then looked down the table, where fingers had replaced utensils. In for a nickel, she told herself, and picked up the little bone and began gnawing on it.

'Sweetest meat is closest to the bone,' Mary claimed.

'Barbecue never tasted this way in Charlotte, did it, Katie?' Eubie asked. He was seated on her left, with his wife just beyond. Katie shook her head in disgust, wishing that he were on her other side so she might kick him one. If ever there was a place for a diplomat, this was it. And Eubie would never fit the bill.

'No,' she acknowledged, and tried to change the subject. But Amanda was not prepared to let her off the hook.

'You must tell me how you came to meet my husband,' she said. 'And what strange—er—coincidence brought you to Harry's house?'

'Katie? You knew Eubie in Charlotte?' Harry sounded both startled and angry.

'Why, yes,' she answered, hoping to smooth things over before Eubie put his big fat foot in his big fat mouth again. 'I was in the *Big Sisters* programme—sponsoring orphan children, you know. Eubie and all the players on the Cougars came down to help work with some of our more difficult cases. I got to know them all fairly well. I would take a few of the children to the ball games, and afterwards Eubie—the players—would buy us all a meal. Win, lose, or draw, so to speak.'

'How charming,' Amanda commented. I wish I had brought my fur coat, Katie told herself. It's getting so cold around here that the words have icicles on them!

'I gather then that you were able to—handle the entire baseball team?' Eloise, with her diamond-sharp tongue. 'And all this time we thought you were just a dear little child!'

'As she certainly is,' Aunt Grace said flatly. 'What a charming idea. And so nice of the players to give their spare time to a worthwhile cause. I congratulate you, Eubie.'

'Yeah,' he grunted, trying to bury himself in a fistful of rib bones.

Harry re-directed the conversation to the planned trip to the World's Fair, and a modicum of calm descended. Aunt Grace quoted by the mile from the travel brochures she had been studying, and Mary entered an occasional counter-point. Katie did her best to disappear into the woodwork, speaking only when spoken to. But with the meal almost over, Mary brought out the strawberry shortcake and the coffee pot. It was then that Katie noticed something that so surprised her she was unable to hold her tongue.

'You're not wearing your engagement ring, Eloise?' The words came out without thought. And all the other conversations around the table stopped. The little blonde woman glared at her down the length of the table, started twice to answer her, and then broke down in tears and ran from the table, upsetting her chair, and her plate of shortcake.

'I thought you were a diplomat,' Harry groaned as he slammed his napkin down on the table and kicked his chair back. 'But you really suffer from Foot-In-Mouth disease, don't you!' He stalked into the house after Eloise.

'Well I—but I—' Katie snatched up her own napkin and used it to hide her tears. The words had burst out before she could think. And now he was off stalking after his lady-love. To comfort her, without a doubt. And just the thought of those strong arms of his wrapped around Eloise was enough to spoil the taste of the dinner.

She mumbled an excuse, backed her chair away from the table, and took off at full speed for the shelter of her room. She sat in her chair by the window, in the dark, and watched the whirl of stars overhead. There was the lost sound of a loon, somewhere in the distance. From the back of the house she could hear occasional laughter as the party went on without her.

Gradually, as the night rolled on into the pit of darkness, and quiet blanketed the outside world, she managed to regain control of her shattered emotions. Mechanically she turned away from the window, struggled to undress, and climbed into bed. It's the only way, she told herself as she settled into the cool comfort of the sheets. It's the only way. I have to get away from him—from here. Somehow or another, I have to get away. Or else I have to snatch him from Eloise, and— the dream that followed hard on her last statement was replete with scenes that caused her to squirm in her bed. Harry King, staked out over an ant-hill, with Katie Russel sitting beside him, smiling sweetly, as she poured little dippers of honey over his arrogant face. Eloise Norris, being stripped by Indian warriors as she ran the gauntlet, only to find that her improper dimensions were all padded, and her beautiful blonde hair was dyed. And then Harry King, lying in bed beside Katie, running his cool hands up over her breasts, and down across her flat stomach, until—

And so it seemed that Katie Russel was the only one in the house besides Jon who got any sleep at all that night—and she rather more than she deserved.

CHAPTER EIGHT

THERE were two crows working off their frustrations outside her window. The raucous argument brought Katie up out of her bed in a hurry. The sun had not yet broken over the mountains behind the house, but there was enough light for her to see by. She struggled up, dressed quickly in a faded blue blouse and a wrap-around skirt, and scrambled into her chair.

The kitchen was empty, but the coffee pot had perco-lated, and it's little red eye glared at her. She snatched a mug of the warm liquid, picking up an apple from the table, and drove out the back door. The patio was a good place to stop for a sip at the coffee mug. She was in no condition to face the multitudes of her enemies, she decided. She pushed the throttle forward and drove off on to the soft wet grass, then around the side of the house, and down to the wire perimeter fence.

Two sheep were busy mowing the grass beside her. She idled along with them, down the perimeter of the plateau, inspecting the quiet valley below. The air was heavy. It seemed to hang over the valley like an invisible cloud. As far to the west as she could see, over the tops of Frozen Knob and Higgins Ridge, the thin black outline of thunderclouds were gathering. Gradually, as the sheep herded her onwards, they moved out of sight of the house, behind the tree-line of the apple orchard.

She called a halt at the point where the little plateau began to turn back into the face of the mountain behind her. The little cove lay quietly before her, everything else blacked out by the surrounding mountain. Below she could barely see the trace of the highway, outlined by its guardian trees. From one or two widely separated points there was a trail of white smoke lifting upwards into the sullen sky. Nothing moved. She watched, entranced, as the sun vaulted up over the top of Big Bald, behind her, and scattered light into the wooded coves below.

It's almost like it might have been for primeval man, she thought. Peaceful, warm, content. Where has that earliest man gone? She relaxed in her chair, picked up her apple, and began to gnaw on her breakfast. The sheep, still clustered around her chair, clumsily settled down to ruminate.

'So this is where you've got to!' The deep bass voice was almost at the level of her ear, so close and caressing that she half-jumped out of her chair. 'Little Bo Peep?'

'Don't be obtuse,' she retorted stiffly. 'What are you doing here?' He bent over her shoulder, so his face blocked out her horizon. She found it impossible to control her trembling fingers. To give them something to do she jammed forward on her drive-control. The little motor below her chair spun weakly, and then stopped.

He moved around to the front of the chair and knelt beside her. 'Why, I've come for my good-morning kiss,' he said.

'After last night's insults?' She tried to keep her voice cool and detached. The little tremolo that slipped in gave her away. He slid one arm around her back, and used the other hand to tilt up her chin. She struggled, but when his lips made gentle contact, she gave up. Weakly, her hands climbed his shoulders to rifle through his hair. Unconscious of what she was doing she parted her lips and tasted the sweet wild honey of him before he broke away, laughing.

'It does seem to work,' he chuckled. 'Well, sometimes. Are you like this with all the men you kiss?' His face was less than six inches away from her, and she could smell the tang of his shaving lotion. Those enormous teeth half-filled her view. Big enough to eat you with! The warning hummed through her partly paralysed mind. 'Well?' he repeated.

'Well what?' she asked feebly. My lord, she screamed at herself, it was only a little kiss. Only a little kiss! You've been kissed before, you fool!

'Are you like that with all the men who kiss you?'

A tiny spark of anger restored her to normality. 'No!' she snapped. 'Are you like this with every woman you meet?'

She seemed to have caught him by surprise. 'Why—no,' he answered slowly. 'You seem to do strange things to me, Miss Russel.'

'Well,' she sputtered, 'I—I would just as soon not have you maul me anymore. I think you take advantage of the fact that I'm tied to this wheelchair!'

He looked down at her with surprise registering on his broad face. Surprise, and—doubt?

'Perhaps you're right,' he half-apologised. 'It just seems to be the only time I can get close to you—when you're out in your chair. Kissed a lot of men, I suppose?'

'None of your business,' she snapped. 'And I don't like yours,' she sputtered at him. She wiped her lips with the back of her hand, trying to obliterate the happening.

'Ah!' he said softly, sibilantly. She felt a thrill of alarm run through her. Why are you such a liar, she asked herself. Why deny him? Why not tell him that you like—everything about him, including his kisses? That you—all her alarm bells went off at once. His hand had casually brushed back the hem of her skirt, and was resting on her knee. It was hard to think. She commanded her own hand to brush his off, but instead it traitorously came to a halt on top of his, and refused to function! Her startled eyes jumped from her knee to his face, but he had turned away, looking down the valley.

She was shaking so much that her teeth chattered. His grip tightened on her knee, as if to soothe. 'Look down there,' he said, as if unaware of what havoc his hand was causing to her shredded senses. 'That's the way it must have looked when my ancestors came over the mountains from Carolina, to settle in the lonely wilderness.

My people were the Over-mountain Men, you know. Scottish, Irish, poor English immigrants, with nothing of their own save a love for land.'

That did it! Lonely wilderness, love for land! Her hands smashed his away from her knee. She shifted in her chair, and smoothed her skirt back in place, her face darkened in anger. This over-proud, arrogant man! He needed taking down a peg or two!

'Hey, what did I say?' he enquired, with a boyish look of innocence on his face. 'My ancestors settled this valley,' he added. 'I'm proud of them.'

'I'll bet you are,' she snapped at him. 'Your fine ancestors came over the mountains because of their love of land, all right—somebody else's land!' She shifted her weight again and glared at him. 'Look, Mr King. When I attended the University of Ohio we had a professor in American History by the name of John Ross. He was a Cherokee from the Western Nation, in Oklahoma. He taught us American history from a very different viewpoint. Let me tell you about it.'

He shrugged his shoulders, apparently in agreement, so she summoned up the rest of her courage and began. 'In the beginning, this land was owned by a people called Paleo Indians,' she lectured. 'We don't know a darn think about them, except that they used flint spearheads, and hunted the bison. Then after them came the Archaic people. There are caves in these mountains whose walls are still covered with their glyphs. We don't know anything about them either, except that they made pottery. Whoever they were, tribes of forest Indians came into the area and displaced them, just as they had displaced the people before them. We don't know much about the Forest people, except that they were hunters and gatherers, and might have been Algonquins. Perhaps Leni Llanape. Are you with me so far?'

'Should I take notes?' he asked sarcastically. 'Will there be an examination after the lecture?'

'Don't be smart,' she snapped. 'Now, what happened

next we do know something about. The Five Nations of the Iroquois came up through these valleys on their way to New York, and smashed the Forest people. Then, directly behind the Five Nations, came the Cherokee Nation, who seized all this land, and chased the other tribes away.'

'At last a familiar name,' he chuckled. 'Continue, professor.'

'So the Cherokee established a civilised nation in this area, beginning just before the time the European started to settle on the coastal plains. The Cherokee lived in towns, were devoted to agriculture, had their own language, and even their own newspapers. And then came the Over-mountain men. And, after a fairly long time, they forced or coerced the Cherokee into leaving. And that's where we are now.'

'I'm sure there must be a moral to the story,' he said.

'There is. The valley of the Tennessee is no different from most of the rest of the world. The original people were displaced, and their displacers in their turn are displaced, and so forth. A good title for a history of almost anywhere in America or Europe would be, "But Nobody Comes From Around Here." And the moral of the story is this. People and cultures are already invading the valley, steadily taking it away from you Over-mountain men. We can only hope that, when your time comes to knuckle down, you will do it with as much honour as the Cherokee did. End of lesson.'

'Well,' he said, after a thinking pause, 'at least you should record that when my people came over the mountains, we bought the land from the Cherokee, and paid them well.'

'Sure you did,' she laughed. 'If you count whisky and blankets a fair price for five million acres of land. If you really believe that, I own a bridge up in Brooklyn I would like to sell to you. But you didn't come down here for a history lesson, Mr King. What is it you really want?'

'Okay, Katie, I'll tell you what I want.'

'What?'

'You, Katie, that's what!'

'For heaven's sakes, don't go on like that. Eloise is making wedding plans for two weeks from now, and you want me?'

'You've got it right!'

'I don't know if you're insane, or Superman, or have a super ego. You want me like you want a hole in your head. What am I supposed to do, change your luck or something?'

'Don't be sarcastic, Katie. It doesn't fit your image. But if you're going to argue, I suppose I can put it off until later. Come on, we'll both get some breakfast!' He walked off towards the house, muttering under his breath, leaving her to follow at her own speed.

She pushed the throttle forward, and swung the wheels of her chair around. Nothing happened. Not even the reassuring click that demonstrated the machinery was working. She tried again, jamming the stick forward as far as it would go. The wheels refused to turn. 'Damn!' she muttered. Both sheep looked around at her, levered themselves up, and walked away.

'You too!' she snarled after them, but they paid her no attention.

Shaking her head in disgust she grabbed the two over-sized wheels and tried to move the chair by hand. It rocked back and forth easily, but refused to move out of the two little ruts into which it had settled. She banged her fist against the arm of the chair, and repeated three or four more of the words her mother had told her never to say. She knew what she had to do, but her pride held her back. She banged the chair arm twice more, and only succeeded in bruising the underside of her fist.

It had to be done. She leaned back in her chair, a look of extreme distaste on her face, and called, rather softly, 'Help.' One of the sheep looked around at her, and a robin, gathering up nerve for the southern flyways, dipped over her head. Using considerably more breath, she started to chant, 'Help! Help! Damnit, he-e-elp!'

Before the last echo bounced off the mountain face behind her he was back. 'You called?' he asked facetiously.

'No, I didn't call—I yelled,' she snarled at him. 'Why couldn't there be some other male around when I need help?'

'There is,' he chuckled. 'Little Jon is just around the bend. You want I should send him to help you?'

'What I really want is a big stick to beat you with!' she told him coldly. 'My chair doesn't work.'

'Ah.' He walked around her surveying the chair from all sides. From out of his pocket he pulled a tiny bulb with wires attached. He kneeled down behind her, out of sight. Something rattled. He got up, brushing grass points from his immaculately pressed trousers. 'Ah,' he told her.

'Ah what?' she asked anxiously. 'Can you fix it? I can't seem to make it go by hand.'

He tucked his little contraption back in his pocket and smiled benevolently at her. 'Tell me, Katie. When you went to bed last night, exactly what did you do?'

'What do you mean, what did—'

'Come on, Katie.' He leaned over and tapped the tip of her nose with his index finger. 'Pay attention now. Watch my lips. What did you do when you went to bed last night?'

'Well, I—I went to my room, and I sat by the window for a while, and then I went over to the bed, and I climbed—'

'No, no, little miss. Details!'

'I—what are you, some kind of voyeur?'

'Details!'

'I—I had a hard time getting undressed, because the cast is so big, but I did, and I put on my nightgown, and I—I pulled back the sheets, and I sort of humped my way from the chair to the bed, and then I fell down on the bed and pulled the blankets up over me, and I—I went to sleep.'

'Leaving the chair standing by the bed?'

'Of course. Did you think I took it to bed with me?'

'What makes the chair go, Katie?'

'I—Electricity. Why are you laughing at me?'

'Because, my lovely maiden, you have to re-charge the battery on that chair every night, by plugging this little wire into the house electric sockets. You're out of electricity, dummy!'

'I'll dummy you if I ever get my hands on you,' she snarled. He immediately stepped within range. She snapped her hands back and settled into the farthest corner of her chair, apprehensive, feeling the changed emotions in the air. He stood there, hands in pockets, looking sombrely down at her. She licked her dry lips, and watched him cautiously.

'Would you—please—' she offered tentatively. 'Would you please push me back to the house?'

'Ah,' he said contentedly. He put his hands to the stainless steel handles at the back of the chair, and began almost effortlessly to push her back towards the house. He was whistling as they went. She sat absolutely rigid in the chair, staring straight ahead, not daring to make a sound.

Instead of pushing her right up to the house, he detoured towards the swimming pool. The sun was high now, the air sullenly warm. He moved the chair into the shade of one of the beach umbrellas set in the concrete of the pool's apron. She half-turned herself to thank him, but he was bending down, plugging the charging cord into the waterproof electric connector some feet away from the pool.

'Now just sit quietly there,' he admonished her. 'The battery will build up a reasonable charge in two hours. And in the meantime I'll get you some breakfast. Gall and wormwood, was it? Or would you prefer scrambled eggs?'

He didn't wait for an answer, but started off across the lawn in the direction of the kitchen. Her hungry eyes followed him lovingly. And what was that interchange all about, she demanded of herself? All we seem to do is peck at each other's pride. Somebody—I—need to be a little bit—a lot, more humble. Her thought was interrupted by a splash behind her in the pool. She squirmed around to look. Baby Jon was splashing away in the middle of the enclosure!

Katie struggled to get up, to do something gallant, but before she could even come upright she saw the flash of another swimmer coming up underneath the baby, and breaking water with an enthusiastic spray. Amanda!

'Oh, my God,' Katie muttered, 'Mine enemies are gathered to smite me!'

But the woman in the pool had turned over on her back, and was gently paddling as she enticed the baby to continue his dogged swim to the near side of the pool. In a moment both baby and mother were sprawled, panting, on the apron.

'Hey, how about that, Katie,' Amanda called. She got up, snatched at a towel from the nearest sun-chair, and swaddled the baby. Both were laughing as they came over to her wheelchair. 'I started to give Jon swimming lessons when he was eight months old,' Amanda said, rubbing briskly at the blond hair just peeping out of the towel. 'I don't know why I waited so late. Mind if we sit here with you?'

'I—No, I don't mind,' Katie mumbled. A quick inspection of the other girl, dressed in a skimpy royal blue bikini, indicated that she couldn't possibly be carrying concealed weapons!

The baby, now dry, settled down on the spread towel and kicked his heels. His mother dragged a sun-lounger over beside Katie and settled back in it.

'I'm not mad at you, Katie,' she said.

'Well, thank goodness for that!' Katie breathed a sigh of relief.

'Eubie and I have been married for four years,' Amanda continued. 'I know him from A to Z. So how far did he get with you?'

'Only to A,' Katie replied. 'He seemed to have forgotten to tell me he was married. A slight oversight.' It was hard to keep the bitterness out of her tone.

'You're pretty lucky,' Amanda nodded. 'He usually aims for Z in a hurry. Is my Adonis getting over the hill?'

'No,' Katie sighed. 'He was in there trying, all the way. When he announced that he was coming back as a "pinch hitter" I packed up and ran—and I only got this far!'

'I heard that part of the story from my brother,' Amanda chuckled. 'He appears to be quite taken with you.'

'Taking, you mean, not taken. He's like an octopus.'

'Men are stinkers, aren't they!'

'All of them,' Katie returned. 'All of them.'

The two women leaned back in their chairs to reflect on the perfidy of the male of the species.

'You—you take it very calmly?' Katie asked.

'My own fault,' Amanda confessed. 'I know better than to leave him alone during the season. But his mother was sick, and she wanted the baby and me to be with her in Nashville. There are times when I think the only solution is to have him neutered. But that would be biting off my nose to spite my face.'

Another period of reflective silence.

'He's a lousy outfielder,' Katie offered.

'Terrible.'

'He needs a peach basket instead of a glove.'

'Or a seeing-eye dog!'

'He told me he would be playing in the majors at Atlanta by next year. They really gave him his release?'

A happy smile broke over Amanda's serious face. 'Yeah!' she exclaimed happily. 'How about that! He's disgusted, but it's beginning to leak through his brain that you can't be a professional baseball player if you can't catch fly balls. No matter how high your batting average is. Isn't that wonderful?'

'I dunno,' Katie commented. 'I like baseball. Eubie was a disaster area. What comes next?'

'Well next,' Amanda said determinedly, 'I encourage him to quit entirely. His father has a string of drugstores in South Tennessee and North Georgia. If I can talk fast enough we'll settle down—in Rossville, maybe—and we'll raise half-a-dozen more kids like Jon, and Eubie can take out his frustrations on the Little League. And we'll all live happily ever after.'

'And if that doesn't work?'

'Then some dark night I'm going to sneak up on him with a sharp knife and alter the shape of his existence!'

Both women laughed. 'I wish I understood your brother as well as you understand your husband,' Katie sighed. 'He overwhelms me.'

'I know what you mean,' Amanda returned. 'But it's all a put-on, Katie. He comes on strong like some extrovert. And he's not.'

'He's not? You could have fooled me.'

'When we were young he was a shy kid,' Amanda mused, 'and Dad was a macho man. Harry hated to mix with people, and showed no interest in the family farm—so when he was eight years old Dad sent him off to a military academy. Can you imagine that—eight years old. He learned to build a wall around himself very quickly. But it's only a wall. Inside him he's still the lonely little introvert he always was. You can tell when he's cracking up. He puts on that big stupid grin, that "well I don't care a nickel's worth" approach, and becomes as brash as brass. But that's all a put-on. He can be easily hurt, Katie. Don't you be the one to do it.'

That was the moment Harry came out, pushing a steaming breakfast trolley. 'Hey, Mandy,' he called. 'Two women laughing? Some poor man is getting the shaft, I'll bet.'

'Something like that,' his sister laughed. '*You* made the breakfast? That's not *you*, brother.'

'Semantics.' He shrugged his shoulders. 'Female chauvinistic semantics!'

'Oh damn,' Katie muttered, more to herself than to the others.

'What happened now?' he inquired.

'I dumped eggs on my skirt,' she sighed. 'It's the only one I've got left. I do most of my living in jeans, but I can't get them on over this darn cast.'

'Now there's a perfect lead-in,' Amanda laughed. 'Harry, you'll take care of Jon this afternoon. Katie and I are going down to Johnson City to buy her a few little things.'

'Hey—just a minute—' he started to complain, and then fell silent. Katie whirled round to see what impossible power had finally shut him up. His sister was glaring at him, jaw stuck out at a furious angle, eyes sparking storm signals. And he had backed down! So that's what it takes, Katie thought. Steel determination! Just wait until the next time he starts fooling around with me!

An hour later he helped them out to the parking lot. 'We'll take the Mercedes,' Amanda calmly ordered. He swept Katie up out of her chair, walked around the car, and put her carefully into the front seat. As Amanda warmed up the engine he folded a lightweight portable wheelchair, and squeezed it into the boot. Amanda reached for the gear stick, but Harry held up a warning hand. 'You just wait a minute,' he called. He walked around again to Katie's window and stuck his head in.

'There's a bus station in Johnson City. And an airport,' he said quietly. 'You *will* come back, Katie?'

She was startled. For the past three hours she had been living in a dream world, all thought of flight abandoned. And now his simple question had brought it all to the fore again. Last night she had sworn that everybody was her enemy. And now Amanda had become a close friend. The problem with Eubie had faded deep into the background. Leaving only—Eloise. 'Is she still here?' she asked. Her upper lip was trembling. 'Eloise, I mean?'

'Yes, she's still here. Trust me, Katie. Come back. Promise?'

'I—I don't know what to say.'

'Just say yes. It's easy.'

'All right,' she sighed. 'But I'm not making any other promises. I'm going to be in Humbersville for my sister's wedding.'

'I understand.' He leaned in closer to her, and dropped a quick kiss on her lips. She was so bemused by the sudden contact that she hardly felt the car move, and she didn't return to the real world until they flashed through Ernestville, at the foot of the mountain.

'We'll have to take the back streets through Erwin,' Amanda commented as they crossed the river and swung up into the quiet residential area. 'Main Street will be a mess. This is the second day of the Apple Festival.'

Katie, huddled up inside herself, barely made a noncommittal comment. Harry King was on her mind. Harry King and Eloise. She pictured them in her mind, Eloise sitting up straight in a plain chair, he standing behind her with one hand on her shoulder. And a big black frame to go around the pictures. Black ribbons. Misery. 'Katie Russel's Dilemma', it would be called. A great photo-masterpiece for all the world to stare at. Damn him! Why couldn't she take him at face value? Harry loves Eloise. Eloise is going to be married—soon! Why was there still this little niggling doubt in the back of her mind? Because only Eloise had said that? But *he* didn't seem to disagree, and Lord knows he had been given ample opportunity.

And yet, every time she turned round, he was after her. And his idea of a kiss was certainly not platonic. Stripping her with his eyes, inviting her. Putting his hand on her knee. What was it with these men? Were Harry and Eubie the same type? Willing to take anything they could get their hands on? Eubie was, for sure. But Harry? Every time he touched her it was as if fire had come into her life. Every time he kissed her she was left totally drained—while he went off whistling, with that inane smile on his face!

'Here we are,' Amanda interrupted her.

'Here we are where?' Katie gasped. As far as she could tell, they were sitting in the middle of a huge parking lot, crowded with cars. 'Is this Johnson City?'

'More or less,' Amanda laughed. 'Hey, times change. Years ago all the big stores were downtown. Today, downtown is a disaster area, and all the big stores have moved out to these shopping malls on the outskirts. This is where I think we'll find the largest selection. Montgomery Wards. No stairs, so we can get your chair around easily. Ready?'

'I'm not sure,' Katie laughed as she opened the door. 'I can't adjust to this weather, and here it is, the first week of October.'

Amanda came around to her side with the wheelchair, and helped her into it. 'It's been unusual this year,' she agreed. 'There are heavy storm-warnings out for this entire area. Thunder storms. That's one of the reasons I want to hurry. Storms in these valleys can be pretty gross. 'She swung the chair around and pushed it up the ramp, into the air-conditioned building.

Amanda pursued shopping the way African hunters go after lions. She moved at high speed, made instant decisions, and moved on. She had accumulated six packages, mostly clothing for herself, before Katie could make up her mind about a single item.

In the end they agreed to split up, Amanda going off to the menswear department, while Katie idled among the thousand-and-one dress racks offered. She finally committed herself to two white cotton blouses, one with a ruffle collar, the other with a detachable front bow. To match the blouses she settled on a burgundy heather stretch-woven skirt, with a back zipper. She had intended to leave it at that, respecting her rapidly shrinking supply of travellers' cheques, until she came across the rack of two-piece units on sale, and lost her heart to a little cranberry set with a ruffled front, long sleeves, and a pleated separate skirt. She was doing arithmetic in her head, fumbling with her wallet, when Amanda caught up with her, and they went out to the car.

They started back under darkened skies. Flashes of lightning could be seen off to the west, over Washington County, but Amanda drove sedately on. They made small talk. Clothes they had bought, or had not. Babies. There was a little touch of envy in Katie's comments about that. The Equal Rights Amendment, and why it had failed to pass the first time. And with it all, as they drifted by miles of apple orchards, a lessening of tensions swept over Katie, a willingness to suspend fact and belief, and to continue to live on dreams. When they came around the bend into Main Street, in Erwin, Amanda brought the car to a halt, and they both laughed until tears came. A little parade was straggling down the street in front of them, an offshoot of something more grand. Booths lined both sides of the street, and from the direction of the Court House Plaza they could hear the sound of amplified country music, roaring over the city.

'I forgot again,' Amanda confessed. 'The Apple Festival. This madness will go on until midnight, or until the thunderstorm breaks it up. Whichever. Want to see a little?'

Outside the parked car, the din had risen to massive proportions. They followed two clowns dressed like red Delicious apples, sampling fare at each of the booths as they passed. Apple dumplings, apple pies, apple jelly, apple jam, apple bread, apple tarts, apples, apple juice, apple sauce, apple cider—there seemed to be no end to it all.

'A once-a-year frenzy,' Amanda chuckled. 'To celebrate the apple harvest, one of the major crops around here. If it doesn't rain too hard or too long, they'll close the street for square dancing after a bit. What's that you're drinking?'

'I don't know. Something apple they had at that last booth. Under the counter, it was. It certainly has cleared my headache. I feel a lot better.'

'You look a lot better, too. Your cheeks are blossoming. You sure you don't know what it is?'

'Well—now that I think of it, the man said apple juice or apple jack, so I took the apple jack. Lovely stuff. There's still a little bit left in my bottle. Want a slug?'

'No wonder you're feeling better,' Amanda roared. 'That stuff is pure dynamite, Katie. It's a brandy, made by distilling apple cider. You're higher than a kite, girl!'

'No such a thing!' she responded valiantly, but her eyes would not quite focus. 'Am I?'

'Yeah, you am, lady. And we'd better get back to the car before they arrest you for driving a wheelchair to endanger.'

They barely made it back to the shelter of the car. Little things seemed so funny. They collapsed on the seat and watched the storm clouds chase revellers off the street, before Amanda managed to jam the key into the starter lock, and the Mercedes began to purr at them.

The drive back up the mountain went slowly, but happily. The massive drops of rainwater smashed at the car, bouncing high off the hood before they disintegrated, and wind tugged at the front wheels and threatened to sweep them off the road. The normal thirty-minute trip took them over an hour, and the setting sun was peeping through breaks in the storm clouds as they pulled up to the gates. There was a fresh-swept smell to the world.

Somebody had been waiting for them. No sooner had Amanda parked the car, then Mary came out, pushing the motorised chair, and directly behind her, Harry. Katie sat still in the car, feeling a bubbling mischief within her, and trying to stifle the hiccups that had just assailed her. Amanda was still laughing.

Harry pulled the door open, kissed Katie very thoroughly, then whistled as he swung her up into her arms and transferred her to the chair. Her usual reaction was tangled up with the hiccups. Her heart beat wildly, she gasped for breath, and her knees rattled. He stood over her with that foolishly amiable smile on his face, watching.

'Don't do that!' she finally mustered up enough breath to say.

'Don't do what?' he asked pleasantly.

'Apple jack,' Amanda tossed in as she strode laughingly up to the house with Mary.

'Don't stare at me like that!' she retorted, and wheeled the chair around. But her momentary anger passed in a cloud of hiccups, and suddenly he became the Perfect Knight. She smiled up at him. He was acting naturally—a pleasant smile, showing those perfect teeth, unruly hair, casual dress, and a smile she could drown herself in. And why shouldn't I take what I can get of it, her confused mind asked. 'To hell with Eloise.' It would have been the perfect statement, but two hiccups interrupted it in its middle.

'What was that about Eloise?' he asked. That deep *basso profundo* voice again. She recalled instantly the night they had met, when, in true operatic style, she had cast the bass as the villain of the piece. 'And to hell with the opera, too!' she said very firmly.

'What in the world are you talking about, woman?' he asked.

'I was just—Harry, if I ask you a very important question, would you give me a straight honest answer?'

'Probably not,' he laughed. 'I learned a long time ago to be careful when dealing with women—especially women who have been drinking apple jack.'

Katie looked around her. Amanda had disappeared into the house, having been met at the door by Jon. Mary was almost at the house, and very consciously trying not to observe what was going on next to the car. So chance it, Katie told herself.

'Harry King,' she said as sternly as she could manage, 'when you kiss me, I go all to pieces. And you know that! Yet all you do is put your hands in your pocket and whistle up some stupid tune. Is that all the effect it has on you? If so, I want you to stop all this nonsense, completely and immediately. You hear me?'

'My, you certainly have worked up a deal of courage,' he laughed. 'Bottled? I can't explain it to you right this minute, Katie. You're not a man, and you'd have a hard time understanding, even if you weren't three sheets to the wind.'

'You don't have to make a Federal case about a few tiny drinks,' she snarled at him. 'I know all about the birds and the bees, and the difference between men and women!' Which was a very long sentence to wedge in between the rapidly increasing hiccups.

'I doubt if you do,' he chuckled. 'Katie, I have the distinct impression that you don't know beans!' And he leaned over to kiss her again, proving his point. But there was troubled concern in the depths of his deep blue eyes.

CHAPTER NINE

ANOTHER week had passed, taking them further into October. Surprisingly the warmth of summer held on, with cloudy humid days, star-lit nights, and a chill only after the sun had ducked behind the western peaks.

'Weather's always a problem at this time of year,' Harry told her. 'We're lucky to have the apple-picking complete in the valley. There've been so many delays that the harvest season north of us may be in serious trouble.'

'What kind of trouble?' Katie asked, out of ignorance. They all turned and stared at her. Even Eloise knows more about apple harvesting than I do, Katie told herself. Dummy! Keep your mouth shut!

'The apple crop is picked mainly by Jamaicans,' Harry explained. 'They are hired in teams for the season. They start in the southern orchards and work their way north. So if one particular area isn't ready, it poses a real scheduling problem for the rest.'

'So there!' Eloise whispered at her as she and Harry left the house.

'Damn!' Katie snarled. It's like walking on eggs, girl. Step carefully, don't you dare break a shell—keep your guard up. Maybe I ought to go home.

Aunt Grace was rubbing her hands with glee as she watched the others disappear. 'Wonderful,' she gushed, 'Our plan is working miraculously!'

'I guess you must be right,' Katie laughed. 'What plan?'

'You know, for goodness sakes,' Aunt Grace said as she struggled with a chair. 'I hate these folding things. You have to be a contortionist to get into them, and a muscle-freak to get out again. You know. Our plan to trap Harry. Katie, you don't have trouble remembering things, do you?' The tiny old woman peered anxiously up at her companion.

'No,' Katie replied, 'I remember well enough. I don't believe it, but I remember. So we're doing well?'

'Significantly. Haven't you noticed that ever since the barbecue Eloise has been almost in hiding? You've scored a million points, my dear.' She rubbed her hands together again. 'Take a look out the window. The pair of them are having a real knock down drag-out fight on the patio. Isn't that wonderful. You'll want to be married in white, of course?'

'Whoa up!' Katie exclaimed. 'Now just wait a darn minute. So we had a good week. That doesn't mean I plan to marry the man. Why he's the most arrogant, pig-headed man in the world!'

'Yes, he is,' Aunt Grace sighed happily. 'Isn't that wonderful? But you'll tame him in time. So wonderful. And next week, when we all are in Knoxville, you'll have plenty of opportunities for advancement.'

'I think there's some misunderstanding. I don't plan to go to Knoxville. There's no way I could get around in those crowds. No way!'

'Of course not, dear. That's the advantage. There'll be you and Harry here, all alone—except for Amanda and Eubie and the boy, of course. Just enough chaperons to meet requirements, and not enough to stop any hanky-panky. Wonderful!'

Katie shook her head. 'There's not going to be any hanky-panky,' she retorted stiffly. 'And I hope you haven't raised that subject with Harry?'

'No indeed, my dear. He always has plenty of ideas of that sort for himself. No need to prime *his* pump. Good work!' She struggled out of the chair, her parchment lips dropped a light kiss on Katie's forehead, and she wandered off, making absent-minded comments about dinner.

Katie wheeled out to the now vacant pool, and settled

herself in her chair. Her eyes caught the flashes of lightning to the west, and the horse-head clouds billowing in a mad rush over Little Bald Mountain. And yet, directly above her head, the sky was brilliant blue. The storm was close; you could feel it. The birds were quiet. Even the grasshopper chorus had disappeared.

A large masculine hand touched her shoulder, and a finger ran through her disordered, wind-blown hair. 'Don't do that, Harry,' she said, but not too severely.

'Oh! Harry is it? And I thought you were *my* girl!'

'Eubie? What in God's name are you doing? Don't you have enough trouble as it is?'

'Me? Trouble?' He laughed as he came round to the side of the chair. He was a big man, but not in the shape and form that Harry was. Eubie was built square from neck to calves, as if someone had started a statue in granite and forgotten to finish it off. 'Amanda and me have no trouble, Katherine. She's mad at me, but she'll get over it. And you're still my girl.'

'You've got to be crazy, Eubie, if you think that I would want anything to do with you. Why is it that you conveniently forgot to tell me you were married? Bad memory?'

'Well, you know how it is. When a fella gets a long way from home, he—'

'I don't know how it is, and I don't intend to find out. You don't deserve a fine woman like Amanda! Somebody ought to fill your south end with buckshot!'

'Now, Katie, that's no way to talk to a close friend!' He moved around in front of her chair now, bending over so his face was a matter of inches from hers.

'What in the name of all that's holy do you think you're doing!' she shouted at him. 'You don't seem to have enough brains to come in out of the rain. And get your hands off me!' Her voice had risen to a shrill shriek as one of his hands pinned her in the chair, while the other stroked her breast.

'One more chance, Eubie,' she threatened him, 'and

I'm going to scream the house down. Get your—' His hand shifted from her breast and clamped across her lips and nose, half-smothering her in the effort. She struggled against his hold, kicking out against his shin with her good foot. He grunted as the sharp point of her shoe bounced off his leg. His hand on her mouth shifted slightly, just enough for her to draw her lips back. With all the power she possessed she bit down on his hand. She could feel the salty taste of blood as he snatched his hand away, howling like a dog.

'You bit me, you damned bitch,' he snarled. He held up his hand in front of her, as if offering evidence. She grabbed at it and bit again.

'Damn! Damn you! Damn!' It seemed to be all he could say. 'And that's my throwing hand, you bitch. I'm gonna wring your little neck and hang you out to dry!'

Up to that moment she had been acting on reflexes, with her eyes half closed. Now she truly opened them and looked. He was standing squarely in front of her, between her chair and the lip of the pool. There was a sullen anger showing on his usually vacuous face. He started to move towards her, both hands outstretched in a clutching grip, aiming for her throat. My God! She told herself. He's really going to do it. He really means to wring my neck! Her hand fumbled for the throttle of her chair, madly trying to back the chair away from his slow, stalking approach. But the chair had only one slow speed backwards, and she knew it would not be enough. Without a second thought, she decided to attack. She jammed the throttle full forward. The big rear wheels whined for a second, then sent the chair hurtling directly at him.

His reflexes were slow. Instead of ducking to one side, he took two steps backwards, teetering on the edge of the pool. By now Katie's fear had turned to anger! Why should she be afraid of this hill-country cracker? Why should he get all the good bits? He was barely holding his balance at the end of the pool, where the deepest water was located. She smiled to herself, and edged the throttle forward again.

The projecting foot rest of the chair caught him a smashing blow just above his ankles. He yelled once, swayed, and then toppled backwards into the water. Katie was unable to sit up straight, so overcome was she in hysterical laughter. So much did she lose control, that she hardly noticed that her chair was still rolling forward. It was not until it tilted forward steeply that she managed to look down and see the green water staring back at her. She barely had time for one deep breath before she and the chair joined Eubie in the swimming pool.

In ordinary circumstances, an unexpected ducking in the pool, even with a cast on her foot, would hardly have affected Katie at all. She relaxed, kept her eyes open, and watched the slow motion development. She and the chair were slowly settling to the bottom. The water was warm, heated by the solar panels. She kept her cool.

When finally one foot touched bottom, she started to push off on the way back up, only to find that her encasted foot was stuck—jammed into the corner of the folding foot rest. She jerked at the foot, trying to dislodge it. A spasm of pain reminded her that the foot inside the cast was still sore. A little more worried now, she bent awkwardly, to examine the problem. Somehow the light aluminium foot rest had become bent, her foot was trapped behind it, and the full weight of the motorised chair was holding her down.

Her breath was running short! Now's the time, she told herself hysterically. Panic! She grabbed the foot rest with both hands, but only succeeded in dragging the chair down on top of herself. She scrabbled at the metal, no longer cool and collected, no longer proud. She looked desperately around her underwater world. Eubie had disappeared. Air was bubbling from her mouth in tiny spurts. A band of pain stretched across her chest. She fought against the easy surrender. All you have to

do is breath in, she told herself. Breath in and drown.
But she fought the urge.

Out of the corner of her eye she saw movement. A
body plunged through the green roof above her, sending
a trail of air bubbles back up in its wake. Strong hands
seized the metal foot rest, wrenching it completely free
from the chair. And then the same strong hands encom-
passed her waist and urged her up, to where the blessed
air awaited. Katie managed to hold on to her senses until
that first sweet gulp of air whistled down into her lungs,
and then she surrendered to the darkness.

'But she's breathing—you don't have to give her the
kiss of life when she's already breathing,' Amanda was
saying, just as Katie wandered back through the fog,
back to life. She just managed to crack one eye open.

'I know I don't,' Harry said. His head leaned over her,
shutting out the light. She could read the deep lines of
concern on his mobile face. His lips touched hers,
lightly, comfortingly.

'Don't,' she said weakly, making a pro-forma com-
plaint which she hoped he would ignore. He did.

'Yes, sure,' he laughed in her ear. 'One more time,
just for luck.' And those tantalisingly comfortable lips
zoomed in on hers again, locked on for a second, and
then withdrew.

'You don't give artificial respiration to girls who faint,'
Mary contributed. 'Seems to me you're funnin' again,
Mr King. Leave the girl alone!'

'Spoilsports!' he announced, in a very aggrieved
voice. But when she opened both eyes he had that inane
grin splattered across his face again. She took two deep
breaths, and struggled to sit up.

'Eubie?' she asked hesitantly.

'Eubie what?' Amanda said sharply. 'Was he mixed
up in this?'

'He—he fell in the water.'

'He fell in the water?' Harry interjected. 'There's a
better word for it than that, Katie. I saw it from the

kitchen window. What was he up to this time? Groping?'

'That's enough,' Aunt Grace intervened. 'The girl's had a shock.' Harry took one quick look at Katie, then stooped and picked her up as casually as if she were a featherweight. She felt suddenly exhausted. She slipped her arms around his neck and nestled her head against his shoulder. The procession trailed after them through the kitchen and into Katie's makeshift bedroom.

'I'll just get these wet clothes off you,' he muttered, and started to work at the buttons of her blouse.

'Harry King!' His hands fumbled to a stop, as Aunt Grace bustled into the room. 'Up to your old tricks? Out of here! Git!'

He hesitated, torn between choices, but finally shrugged and ambled out the door. 'Now then,' his aunt crooned, 'out of these wet things, a good brisk drying with a warm towel, and something to drink.'

'I'm all right,' Katie protested. 'The only thing that trouble me is how angry I got. Boy, I haven't lost my temper that wildly since Caesar was a pup! How is Eubie?'

'That one!' Aunt Grace's noise crinkled in disdain. 'He got a good ducking, that's for sure. But that's only half of what he's got coming to him. Amanda led him upstairs by the nose! And Harry—well! Did you see that look in Harry's eyes when he went out? Eubie Fairfield had better be hard to find, believe you me.'

As she talked her fingers were busy stripping Katie to the skin, and now she busied herself with a huge bath towel, drying her, and restoring her circulation at the same time. 'Sit up now,' she commanded, 'and let me do your back.' The door opened, and Eloise came in, carrying a tray, and fresh towels.

'Katie?' the blonde woman said as she came up to the bed. 'I've brought you some sassafras tea. It's good and hot!' Katie looked up at her through the fringe of her disordered curls. There was something different about Eloise. The hard shell had cracked. She looks real instead of artificial! Katie accepted the tea-cup and sipped gratefully at the hot liquid. Eloise came around to the other side of the bed, wrapped Katie's hair in one of the fresh towels, and began a gentle drying motion. The treatment was soothing, calming. Aunt Grace had finished her part of the work, and stepped back to admire.

'You really are a lovely girl,' she commented. 'Now, let me see—I know. Harry's robe! I'll be back in a minute.' She walked out the door. Eloise continued her ministrations, then picked up another towel and wrapped Katie's hair up in a turban.

'It's dry enough to stop dripping,' she commented. 'I'll bring you a blow-drier in a minute.'

'Thanks, Eloise,' Katie said softly. 'If I were in your position I would have torn the hair out by the roots, you know. What's happened?'

'The inevitable,' the older woman sighed. 'You really are a nice kid, Katie. I've held out as long as I could, but it's too late to change now.' She sat down in the chair next to the bed and folded her hands. Why, this is the first time I've ever seen her relax, Katie told herself. Always before she has appeared to be wound up like a too-tight clock spring, ready to snap at any moment. And now she is leaning back against the chair, at rest.

'Have you ever been scared, Katie?'

'Who hasn't! What brought that on?'

'No, I mean really scared. Really.'

Katie squirmed round in the bed to look at her visitor. The woman was looking up at the ceiling, twisting her hands together, biting her lip. There was a glimmer of tears in her eyes.

'Yes I have, once or twice,' Katie replied. 'And you?'

'I—I'm scared all the time. That's my problem. Everything scares me. I'm scared of meeting people, and not meeting people. I'm scared of being as poor as we were when I was young. I'm scared of thunder. I'm scared of most anything, I guess. That's why I've always worn a hard-case exterior.'

'Well, you could have fooled me, Eloise. You don't look it.'

'No, I've learned over a lot of years to hide everything, even from myself. I work in a tough business, and I'm scared to death of it too. But I have to eat, so I hide my feelings, and keep at it. Lord, I'm tired of hiding. You know the only safe place for a scared woman?'

'No, what?'

'Being married, Katie. That's the only real refuge. Don't keep fighting for something you can't have. Find a man who will take care of you, and marry him. That's the only way.'

'Even if you don't love him?'

'You could learn to love. Or at least I could. I'm sorry I've been such a pain to you, Katie. You're really a good kid. I wanted Harry. We've had some dreadful fights but I still thought I could hold him to his promise. Until I saw him come out of that swimming pool with you in his arms. That's when I knew it was all over. The look in his eyes as he watched you. Well, I'm not too clever, but I don't have to be hit with a meat axe. I've already called Giles, in Atlanta. If I'm lucky, he'll never know he was second-best. I'll go rustle up that hairdrier. Good luck to you, Katie.' Eloise got up from the chair and walked out of the room without looking back. Katie sat up and hugged her knees against her breasts.

Now what in the world was that all about, she asked herself. And who is Giles? I think I must have been right the first day I tumbled into this crowd. None of them have all their marbles!

They ate in the kitchen that night. It was a subdued group that gathered around the table to share beef stew, rampant with fresh vegetables, and deep-dish apple pie. The smell of fresh-baked bread filled the whole house.

'Where's Amanda?' Katie asked through a mouthful of hot bread.

'Gone,' Mary said. 'Packed up, bag and baggage, and

drove off while you was changin' clothes.'

'Why, Harry?' Katie asked.

'They've gone to Chattanooga,' he said. 'They have a home there. Amanda has decided to give it one more try. She said to give you her apologies and her love.

'And Eubie?'

'He didn't have anything to say.'

'Well, of course he didn't,' Aunt Grace interrupted. 'How could he? That was a terrible thing that you did, Harry. He was a guest in the house. You shouldn't have hit him so hard. He'll lose all those front teeth. You wait and see!'

'I don't intend to see,' Harry snarled. 'If I ever see him again he'll lose the rest of them. If it wasn't for the fact that my sister married—well, I would have killed the bastard!'

'But it wasn't all that bad,' Katie interjected. 'I could have handled the whole affair. You needn't have made a Federal case out of it. After all, I pushed *him* into the pool, not the other way around!'

'I didn't hit him because he pushed you into the pool,' he snarled at her. 'I hit him because after you fell in he just sat on the side of the pool and didn't move a muscle to help. Do you realise that in another two minutes you could have been—Damn you, Katie Russel, why did you ever come into my life! You and your damn schemes!' He scraped back his chair, threw his napkin on to the table, and stormed out the door.

'Well!' Mary commented.

'Well indeed.' Aunt Grace sounded highly pleased about the whole affair. 'Didn't I tell you, Katie?'

'Maybe we'd better talk about something else,' Katie suggested.

'I know what,' Mary laughed. 'Tell us about your home in Ohio. Did you really live on a farm?'

'And feed the pigs and all that?' Eloise asked.

'Who me?' Katie laughed. 'I don't know how that rumour got started. Admittedly Humbersville is a small town, but not a farm town. Steel mills is what we raise. And my family lived in the best part of town. Dad's photo studio was a gold mine. Could I have another piece of that pie?'

'Want ice cream on top of it?'

'I—' Whatever she had planned to say was blasted out of her mind. Harry banged his way through the kitchen and out of the back door with a tool box in his hand. The heavy door swung shut behind him with a rattle that shook the back wall of the house, and the screen-door added a postscript. Aunt Grace walked over and peered out the window.

'He's going down to the swimming pool,' she announced. 'There is hardly enough light out there to see the water. I haven't seen Harry so mad before in all his life.'

'Pay him no mind,' Mary said gleefully. 'It's his conscience bothering him.'

'Well, it's not on my account,' Eloise commented. She got up from the table and stretched her voluptuous frame. 'And me for the high road.'

'You're leaving now?' Katie exclaimed.

'I told you,' the other girl responded. 'I like driving at night. I'm on my way to Atlanta to meet a wedding party. Good luck to you, Katie. Be happy. Thank you, Aunt Grace, for a great deal of hospitality. You all take care of Harry. He's a whole lot of man.' She walked out the door. A few minutes later they heard a car start up and drive away.

'Well, I'll be horsewoggled!' Aunt Grace said. There was a dazed expression on her face. 'She gave up!' The old lady grinned as she got up from her chair and danced a little jig. 'And now the field is clear, Katie. Move in for the kill!'

'Move in for the—what?'

'Katie, are you sure there are no dim-witted people in your family? Get out there now, soothe him down, make your play!'

'I—I wish I knew what you were talking about, Aunt Grace.'

'I'm talking about you and Harry. Harry and you. Whatever way you want to put it. Now's the time. Strike while the iron is hot! What other clichés are there? Get out there and give in gracefully!'

'Aunt Grace? You mean that? I should—surrender?'

'Of course I mean that. Want me to push you out there?'

'No. No! You don't know what he wants from me. I do!'

'Of course I know what he wants. He wants to marry you. Get with it girl, before the moment passes.'

'Aunt Grace, that's not what he wants!'

'Don't argue with me, girl. Get out there. No, wait. You need to give him a domesticated picture. Where's that embroidery you've been working on? Mary, be a dear and go get Katie's sewing bag.'

'But I—I can hardly embroider in the daylight, never mind pitch darkness!'

'It's only a prop. You can tear it all out tomorrow. Ah, here it is. Now, out with you!'

She was still in a state of panic when she found herself outside on the patio, the kitchen door closed behind her, and nothing in front but the single light at the poolside, against which ten million insects were already hurling themselves in glee. She shrank down in the wheelchair, wishing with all her heart that some miracle might come to pass and relieve her of all this—commitment. But God, in His infinite wisdom, did nothing. Katie straightened up, and began to manoeuvre the chair in the general direction of the pool.

Twice her canvas sewing bag slipped to the ground, and she had to stop to retrieve it. Her moistened palms kept slipping on the wheels, as she used unaccustomed muscles to move the chair over the grass. At least I won't drive *this* chair into the water, she told herself. Eventually she crossed the terrain, and came up behind him. He was working on some electrical connection in the box on one of the light poles. Just by looking at his back she could tell he was still angry. He held himself stiffly, with squared shoulders. If he turns around, she whispered to herself, he'll be Torquemada! I just know it. There will be a stake, and a condemnation, and an *auto-da-fe*. And that will be the end of Katie Russel. Should I speak? Or maybe cough? Better not! Instead she set the hand-brake on her chair, watched his busy fingers for a moment, then delved into her bag for the big red burgundy tablecloth she had been embroidering for sister Margarita's wedding.

She hardly remembered where she had stopped with the tablecloth, it had been so long ago. Although there was plenty of thread, all the needles seemed to have disappeared. Keeping her eyes on his busy back she fumbled in the depths of the bag.

'Damn!' she muttered when she found the first needle. Point upwards, of course. She sucked at the blood leaking from the top of her forefinger, and wished mightily that she were in Humbersville, Ohio—or Norman, Oklahoma, for that matter. Anywhere—else.

From the little hut built near the corner of the pool she heard a small motor grind and grind, and then start up with an enthusiastic roar. At which point the man in front of her stood up straight, and slowly turned around. 'Domestic scene, right from the script?' he enquired casually.

'I—well—yes.' She ducked her head, and vainly tried to thread the needle.

'For crying out loud,' he said sarcastically. 'Didn't they even teach you how to thread the needle?' He relieved her of both needle and thread, and in three spare movements ran the thread through the proper hole. 'Like that,' he continued, handing it back to her.

She huddled down in her chair, doing her best to disappear and still be in plain sight. He had both hands in his pockets, whistling that damnable tune she still could not identify. In self-protection she picked up one corner of the heavy cloth and began to fill out the pattern.

The thump of the needle as it pulled through the cloth offered some small comfort. She took a deep breath, and worked faster. So he was sarcastic! So he was obnoxious! At least he hadn't tried to hit her. And that seemed a tremendous improvement over his attitude at the table when, she was sure, he was just about to wind up and whack her one on her—someplace. She pushed the embroidery needle at high speed, watching him out of the corner of her eye.

He went back to the electrical box, checked something, and came back to her, carrying a folding chair with him. He set it up just beside her, and sat down. For several minutes there was only the chuffing of the motor, and the thump of the embroidery needle.

'Christmas present?' he asked.

'No,' she replied cautiously. 'Wedding present.'

'For somebody I know? Marion?'

'No. Margarita, my other sister.'

'What's the wedding date?'

'December 15th.'

'You think you're going to make it on time?'

'No—I—I guess not.'

He lifted up the burgundy cloth and scanned it carefully. 'I don't see why not,' he chuckled. 'You've got almost three months, and it's almost two-thirds done.'

'Yes.'

'Yes? Yes, but no? What's the catch?'

'Oh, why do you have to be so darn perfect!' she muttered at him. 'I know it won't be on time. The wedding date was December 15th, two years ago! I sent them a picture of it, and promised I'd finish it—some day. I procrastinate a lot.'

'Ah. This whole thing begins to smell like a stage manager is in the wings. Well?'

'Yes,' she confessed.

'You and the Old Witch. The conspiracy?'

'Yes,' she sighed. She secured the needle in the corner of the pattern and carefully folded it all up. Putting it back in the sewing bag, she set the container on the concrete apron and folded her hands.

'You're not too—angry?' she asked.

'Not too,' he responded. 'It was a pretty stupid plot, after all. Nice out here at night, isn't it? All those thunderheads are sticking to the valley.'

'Mmm. Nice,' she said. 'What's the motor doing?'

'Pumping out the swimming pool. It was almost time to do it anyway, but when your chair went into the pool, all the acid in those batteries leaked out. It's too diluted to hurt anybody, but we wouldn't want to swim in it. When I get the pool pumped out I'll get your motorised chair back, and see what we can do with it.'

'I feel like a fool, causing you all this trouble. I've been nothing but trouble to you since I arrived. I think I'd better go home?' She had meant it to be a statement, but it came out a question, and ended as a plea. She shifted in her chair to look at him, but the floodlight was at the wrong angle, and he was cast in shadows.

'I don't think so,' he replied, after a brief silence.

She gave a little sigh of contentment, and settled back in her chair. They were both staring straight ahead, watching the level of the water in the pool slowly drop. From the distant valley she heard the wail of a double-diesel locomotive. When the echo died out, the light, sweet song of a nightingale followed.

'Eloise—' she started to say, and then stopped. He turned and looked at her. 'Eloise is gone,' she whispered.

'Yes,' he returned. 'Shall I tell you about her now?'

'You don't have to, Harry,' she hurried to say.

'I'm glad I don't have to,' he answered, 'but I will anyway. I told you that she started out as a share-cropper's daughter. Here in the south, that's what's known as being dirt poor. She fought her way up near the top in a dog-eat-dog profession, but it was obvious that she could never hang on. So she opted for marriage. She became engaged to a dear friend of mine, who unfortunately was killed racing cars. Before he died, my friend asked me to take care of Eloise. She was there when I promised. Somehow or another she decided that I had promised to marry her. She really came apart at the seams, and worked up a fixation on me. But marriage was never in the cards for us. I introduced her to an old schoolmate of mine, a fellow who's made a buck in textiles down in Georgia. But Eloise had no confidence. She felt that she needn't commit herself to anything, because I would always be there. So, she fumbled around for almost a year, and then you came along—and spoiled everything for her. I finally had to tell her point-blank that I couldn't play her game any longer. So she squeezed up her courage, called Giles, and she's gone off to marry him. Satisfied?'

'Oh yes,' she answered happily. Oh yes, indeed! Good luck, Eloise. Be happy. Have a ball, and six kids. Or none, if that's what you want. Bless your marriage—as long as it isn't to Harry!

'What are you thinking?'

'Nothing—nothing much. I thought I ought to get Eloise a wedding present. A very expensive wedding present!'

'Ah!'

'You do think that—that Eloise and Giles—they'll be—happy? You would want your old school friend to be happy, wouldn't you?'

'Don't be a romantic, Katie. I said Giles and I went to school together, not that we were friends. They're two of a kind, that pair. They deserve each other!'

'Oh! What a cruel thing to say!'

'Come off it, Katie. Whatever did Eloise do for you that was nice?'

'She went away?'

'And that's enough small talk,' he muttered. He snatched her up out of the chair and settled her on his lap. She nestled herself against the wool of his light sweater, squirming to get as close as possible. His chin came down on top of her head. One of his arms was round her back, with his huge hand firmly set against her ribs, just below the swell of her tiny breast. The other hand dropped to her lap, and imprisoned her free hand. Her other was cuddled up between them, hard against his throbbing heart. She waited, almost holding her breath, for something else to happen. Nothing did.

Oh well, she told herself, I'm here! It's a wonderful place to be. Even if nothing else ever happens, I'm here for a time, just where I want to be. I wonder what Mama would say? Or Grandmother? I've got him just where he wants me! I wonder if he wants me here, or just wants me? Our children are bound to have red hair. Bound to!

'It's a lovely old place,' he murmured into her hair. 'And I'm the last of the Kings. I wonder what will happen to it all?'

'You're bound to have children,' she suggested hopefully.

'I'm not too sure,' he returned softly. 'I'm not really the marrying kind.'

'Oh? What kind are you?'

'Love 'em and leave 'em,' he chuckled. 'Or at least that's my track record so far. You're very soft, Katie.' One of his hands had slipped into the gap between her blouse and her skirt, and was wandering over the smoothness of her stomach. She stopped breathing.

'Oh me,' he snorted. 'So much for my weather predictions. Here comes the rain!' He jumped up and transferred her back to the wheelchair, then piloted her speedily towards the house. They barely made it to the kitchen. They were travelling so fast that the screen door slammed into the side of Katie's cast, and when they were finally safe and dry she looked down at it.

'Harry,' she exclaimed. 'I'm coming to pieces. I mean, my cast is coming to pieces!' He squatted down beside the chair and ran a finger over the edge of the cast.

'Plaster of Paris,' he announced. 'When you got it wet in the pool the whole thing started to disintegrate. We'll have to take you down to the hospital tomorrow and have the People Mechanic do something about it.'

'I think I'm bad luck,' she said soberly. 'Everything I touch seems to turn to—marmalade.'

'Don't let it worry you,' he offered. 'We have to go to Johnson City tomorrow anyway. The girls are going off to the World's Fair. We'll drive them to the airport, then stop by the hospital and get an overhaul, or something. But that's an early start. I'll get Mary to help you to bed, Katie, and we will take up this discussion at a later date.'

At a later date! She mulled that one over in her mind as Mary helped her out of her clothes, and into a nightgown. As she brushed her hair, she considered. Eubie was no longer a problem, at least not for her. Poor Amanda. Eloise had eliminated herself from the competition. Poor Eloise. Somehow or another she pictured a great big score-board, in some baseball park she had known. In big flashing numbers it read, 'Harry King 2, Women 0.' *But I'm not a marrying man.* And with that one phrase he had eliminated Katie Russel from the competition, too. Poor Katie Russel! An uninvited tear streamed down her cheek.

'Hey, Katie,' Mary said, 'You're crying?'

'I must have brushed too hard,' she lied. 'I think I'm getting a headache.'

'I'll bet you know an old gypsy remedy for that, don't you?' The younger girl's face lit up in anticipation.

'Oh sure,' Katie sighed. 'All we need is about six ounces of lady slipper roots. We boil them for four hours, strain the water, and let it cool. If you drink four ounces every six hours it does the trick!'

'But we don't have any lady slippers,' Mary mourned. 'I haven't seen any since last spring.'

'Well, in that case, maybe a couple of aspirins,' Katie suggested. 'And then I'll get to bed.'

CHAPTER TEN

A COLD front moved through the valleys during the night, and the sun popped up to a true mountain morning. A north wind, with a nip in it, rustled the serried ranks of trees on the mountain, scattering the smoke trails from uncounted hidden house. Occasionally a gust shook the old house, and it creaked like a ship in heavy seas. Katie opened one eye gently, then remembered that this was a travel day, and no one could be spared to help her dress. She scrambled into her chair and wheeled herself into the bathroom, where a brief wash in the hand basin had to make do. Then back to the bedroom, where she struggled into briefs, a half-slip with a camisole top, and the new cranberry blouse and skirt set which she had just purchased. The cast bothered her. It was beginning to disintegrate in an alarming manner, so that sliding into her cotton briefs had been an adventure rather than a discomfort. She pushed herself to her feet so her skirt could fall normally, then settled back in the chair and started for the kitchen.

Everyone was waiting for her. Aunt Grace smiled at her as Mary and Harry busied themselves with the food. 'Hurry up, Katie,' she coaxed. 'His High Mightiness is off on one of his growling moods, and we all have to be in the car in fifteen minutes, or else!'

'Or else what?' Katie asked, still not quite awake.

'Or else the sky will fall, Chicken Little!' The old lady giggled into her cup of coffee. Katie shook her puzzled head and poured herself a mug of the brew. Obviously that was all she was going to be told, she mused. Or perhaps I should put my foot down and refuse to go. Wouldn't that be a good thing? Sure it would. I'd put my foot down, and he'd break it, and then I would have casts on both feet, and —oh lordy, she sighed to herself, why

149

am I so confused? I'm over twenty-one, and I've been around, so to speak. I wouldn't be surprised if I've kissed more boys than he has girls—well, perhaps not all *that* many. But what I need to do is to—love 'em and leave em? Why that rotten—

'Daydreaming, Princess?' The deep bass voice was right in her ear. She jumped, startled, and succeeded in spilling her coffee all over her skirt.

'Damn you, Harry!' Her teeth were clenched tight to suppress an outburst. 'Now I'll have to change my skirt. Why do you always pussyfoot up on me like that?'

'Me? Pussyfoot?' He looked down at her in injured dignity. 'Mostly because you keep daydreaming, Katie Russel. And the devil you'll change. We haven't the time. Air flights won't wait.'

All of which made him ten times more angry as she took another fifteen minutes to replace her skirt, and then decided to change her blouse too, just to teach him a lesson. By the time she manoeuvred her chair out to the car he was mumbling to himself, and occasionally to the other two very interested women—who were doing their best to appear uninterested.

'Well, get in,' he roared at her.

'I have to take my chair with me,' she responded primly.

There was another explosion of mumbling, but he climbed out of the driver's seat, slammed the door as if he were buying a used car, and stomped around to the back, where he folded up her chair and dropped it into the capacious boot of the Mercedes. On his insistence she shared the front seat with him, leaving Aunt Grace and Mary to rattle around in the spacious back seat. The front seat was roomy too, but somehow Katie had considerable difficulty maintaining a space between herself and the driver. It was not until they flashed up to Erwin that he relaxed. And her problems were amplified.

'You can't shift gears with my knee,' she hissed at him.

'Of course not,' he returned in an undertone. 'It's an

automatic-drive car.' Despite his assurances, the hand was not removed. She sat tense, and yet somewhat pleased as the big car moved along. After all, she told herself, there's a certain amount of comfort to be had from this outright display of male chauvinism, providing the ladies in the back don't see it. But both of *them* were busy scanning the white earth of the abandoned Feldspar mine, just outside Erwin, at that moment, and didn't seem to notice.

They arrived at the Johnson City Airport without incident. Instead of stopping at the passenger terminal, he drove them out on to the concrete tarmac, and parked by a waiting Cessna 180. The travellers were unloaded, and goodbyes quickly said.

'I'll see you after my operation,' Mary said cheerfully. Katie made affirmative noises, knowing that she would be long gone before the lovable girl returned.

'Don't worry about it,' Aunt Grace told Mary. 'I had a dream about Katie last night. Dreams never lie. She'll be here, waiting. Dream never tell you false!'

Harry muttered something under his breath, something that sounded suspiciously like 'Oh, don't they?' But that was the moment when the pilot of the Cessna gunned his engine for a run-up test, and in moments they were moving out to the end of the runway, tailing a US AIR 727.

'They'll be in Knoxville before we get home,' Harry grunted. 'It's only a little over a hundred miles by air. Hop in.'

She had been just outside the car, leaning on his arm all this time. It had hardly seemed important to get her chair out for such brief goodbyes. But when he helped her into the seat she huddled as far away from him as possible, clutching at the door latch as if she were some parachute jumper, waiting for the green light. He walked around the big Mercedes, and settled down in the driver's seat with a sigh.

'Well,' he said, 'alone at last!' He reached into the

pocket of his suede jacket and pulled out a cigarette case. 'Mind if I smoke?' he asked.

'Yes, I do,' she snapped. 'I mind a great deal!'

For once, she could see, she had penetrated the mask he presented to the world. He sat there for a moment, the silver cigarette case half-opened. Then, shaking his head and sporting a wry smile, he dropped the cigarette back into the case, snapped it closed, and reached over towards her to drop the case in the glove compartment. As his arm grazed her lap she shrank as far away as she could get. He pulled himself erect and stared at her, his heavy eyelids beetling a cold look of appraisal in her direction. He started to say something else, then thought better of it. He put the key in the lock, started the engine, and drove out of the hangar area with a squeal of tires. She stayed in her corner, huddled up against the cold metal of the door handle. How could she explain to him that—very suddenly, just moments ago—she had remembered that she was going back up the mountain with him to the house, where they would be *alone* together for Lord knew how much time!

The drive back to Erwin went in complete silence. She kept her eye resolutely on the scenery outside the window, chuckling once at the antics of a group of youngsters who were dismantling one of the street booths from the Apple Festival. When they turned into Sinasta Drive, just before they reached the hospital, he pulled the big car over to the curb and stopped.

'Okay,' he said, 'what's the problem?'

'I—what problem?' she squeaked.

'What problem! We've driven seventeen miles, and all that time you've said not one word.'

'But Harry—'

'But Harry—' he mimicked in a falsetto voice.

'That's not fair, Harry!' She sat up straight and glared at him. 'You told me yourself that you didn't like gabby women! All I've been doing is just what you told me to!'

'Oh!' he had that broad grin on his face again. 'That's

the last thing in the world I ever expected from you, Katie. Sometimes I don't say exactly what I mean. You could have said a word or two here and there. Just so you don't babble. Do you always plan to do what I tell you to?'

'And that's not fair, either, Harry,' she said firmly. 'I've been honest with you. Can you say the same?'

'Aha,' he retorted. 'Not to change the subject, let's get that cast of yours fixed.' He started up the engine, and drove the heavy car up to the entrance.

While Harry was taken aside to fill out forms, Dr Foreman whisked Katie into one of the vacant examination booths and knelt down in front of her to examine the damage.

'Yes,' he concluded, 'it has to be changed. Whatever made you decide to go swimming with a cast on your foot?'

'I didn't decide,' she told him grimly, 'It was more like a—a spontaneous idea. Me and my wheelchair!'

'Oh? The chair went in too? How about that!' He chuckled as he picked up his little electric saw and split the cast down its side. She could feel the instant relief as the pressure was removed from the uninjured segments of her leg and foot. The doctor smiled at her, and applied a small amount of skin cream to the uncovered areas.

'Itches like the devil, doesn't it?' he commented, as his gentle fingers massaged the area. 'Got a bad temper, have you? He's a good man.'

'What in the world are you talking about?' she gasped.

'I've known Harry, man and boy, for twenty-five years,' he returned. 'Sometimes he's not very articulate—especially when he's serious and doesn't want anyone to realise. He's a good man, for all that.'

'Maybe,' she sighed. 'But you're not a woman.'

'He's still a good man.' He got up to punctuate the conversation. 'Now, we'll have you up to X-ray for another picture. Then perhaps we could put a walking cast on your foot. That doesn't mean that you go walking on it, you know. Crutches will be the name of the game!'

Two hours later they were back in the car. She turned her new plaster boot back and forth, admiring its smallness more than its shape.

'Henry says you still have to take it easy,' Harry reminded her. Those were the first words he had addressed to her since they entered the hospital.

'I know,' she returned. They had turned around and were going back the way they had come, back towards Johnson City.

'This isn't the way home—way to your house,' she objected.

'Not yet,' he returned. 'We have a couple of prescriptions to fill. My favourite drugstore is down on Main Street.' He manoeuvred the big car down Gay and parked at the corner of Main, where a big REXALL sign advertised everything from prescriptions to patent medicines, from candy to cosmetics, and, of course, the inevitable soda fountain and sandwiches. Everything a normal American drugstore would carry. 'Wait for me,' he said as he opened his door.

Sure, wait for me! What the devil did he think I was going to do, run all the way back to Charlotte? If only he were not so casual about the whole thing! Wait for me. I'm not the marrying kind. For the first time in Katie's young life a thought ran through her mind—'and maybe I'm not either?' What would it be like if she offered him what he really wanted? Suppose—just suppose, when we go back up the mountain, he asked me to—to do it, and I said yes. A delicious shiver ran up and down her spine. Her imagination ran riot, spurred by an almost complete lack of facts and experience. She substituted fiction where fact was not available, and embroidered on things she thought might be true. There was a vacuous smile on her face when he came back. Her mouth was half open, and her tongue glided sensually over her full lips.

'Katie?' He shook her shoulder gently. His touch snapped her out of her fantasy. She was breathing too fast, unable to completely control her dream-reaction.

Almost unconsciously she leaned towards him as he settled in behind the wheel, lifting her glowing face up to him, eyes sparkling.

'Well!' he muttered in astonishment. He slid over in the seat, wrapped one big arm around her shoulders, and gently kissed her. The shock of contact finally penetrated her mental curtains. With a gasp almost of terror she withdrew, crowding over against the door again, breaking out of his gentle grasp.

His arm dropped to the seat as those deep eyes surveyed her huddled form. 'I *did* think you were offering,' he said sarcastically. 'Excuse *me*!'

He moved over behind the wheel and put the key to the ignition. 'I don't understand why you're so jumpy, Katie,' he prompted.

'I don't want to talk about it,' she replied. 'Can't we just—just find something else to talk about?'

'You bet. What?'

'It's a—a nice town, Erwin.'

'City,' he replied caustically. 'City. Almost five thousand people live here. Yes, it's nice.'

'All farmers, I suppose?'

'Oh no. There's a small but growing factory base in the area. A couple of industrial parks, a nuclear research facility, railroad offices, that kind of thing. How about the weather—that's an innocuous subject. Or would you prefer to tell me the name of the subject that we're *not* going to talk about, and then I won't have to be so careful.'

'All right, Harry.' She faced straight ahead, smoothed down the wrinkles in her skirt, and licked her lips nervously. 'When we go home—when we get to your house,' she amended, 'we're going to be all alone. Just the two of us. Nobody else. Amanda won't be there. Just you and me.' She looked over at him quickly, screening her face as best she could behind her curls.

'There's nothing wrong with your arithmetic,' he responded, 'but your English is terrible. Just you and I—'

'Don't pick nits,' she snarled at him. 'You and—we'll

be all alone in that house, ten miles from any neighbour. I don't think my mother would approve!' He started to say something but she held up her hand to stop him. 'But if I do stay there is to be no more of this kissing and touching, and things like that, and that's what we're not going to discuss. You hear!'

'Ah. So that's the problem,' he said solemnly, looking suddenly like a wise old owl. She looked over at him again, just in time to catch the gleam in those deep blue eyes of his. 'Very well, Katherine Russel. I, Harry King, do solemnly swear that when we get home I will not kiss you or touch you or things like that—until you ask me to.'

'Fat chance that'll happen!' She concentrated on the view at her side of the car, where a couple of workmen were cleaning up the gutters. She had to do something with her hands. She gave her tight mass of curls a whirl or two, and then began to use her fingers as a comb. What did he mean by that, she thought. Unless you ask me to? What was the catch? There was bound to be one some-where in that pile of words. He was too cunning and devious to give up so easily. Too much of a hunter for me to believe that this particular lion was willing to lie down with this particular lamb, and not make a barbecue out of it! Until you ask me to? As if it were a foregone thing, and only the exact time was in debate? Could he *make* her want to kiss him? Well, if he did it once, she knew she would not be able to stop him a second time. Or should she have said she knew she would not be able to stop *herself* at the second one? And the third. And whatever. But if she could avoid that first one, she had a fighting chance!

'Well,' he interjected, 'can we continue this United Nations debate while we're driving home? This is a bad place to park.'

'Don't make fun of things you don't know anything about,' she reprimanded him.

'Okay, okay,' he chuckled. 'I apologise for my ignor-ance, and any other stupid male statements I might make in the next half hour. Can we go?'

'Yes, we can go,' she told him flatly. 'You need to do a lot of apologising. You have a lot of ignorance, and a very great deal of arrogance. I don't think my grandmother would approve of you at all.'

He started the engine and swung the big black car back up the street to pick up US 19S. 'Grandma, huh,' he mused. 'A tough old bird?'

'You'd think so if you met her, Harry. When my father died he left me some money—in Grandmother's trust—until I got married, or became thirty. So, in a sort of way, Grandma is my guardian. She'd chew you up and spit you across the Ohio River, Harry King!'

'How about that,' he said. 'If we get married we'll have to keep out of her range. Is it a lot of money?'

'No. Of course not. What was that you said?'

'I said we'd have to keep out of her range.'

'No, I mean before that. Just before that!'

'I don't remember exactly. I meant to indicate a certain amount of caution when dealing with your—oh, I see what you mean. I said if we get married.'

'But—I don't remember anything being said about us—getting married. Except for your aunt. Aren't you the one who loves 'em and leaves 'em? Isn't that what you said?'

'Now, Katie, I can't be called on to remember everything I've ever said, you know. All I'm suggesting is that, although I prefer my bachelor life, I'm willing to let you try to convince me. What could be fairer than that?'

'You really are an egotistical man,' she said stiffly. 'For the record, I'm not going to marry you. I am going home to Ohio for Marion's wedding, and in between that time and this, there's really nothing important that I want to say to you!'

'Are you mad because I didn't ask you nicely, Katie? It's pretty hard to do the *down-on-one-knee* bit in a car. And besides, you've got to convince me yet.'

'Take my answer as final, then,' she snapped. 'No, I

won't marry you. No, I won't try to convince you otherwise. There's more to getting married than—than just
hopping into bed. I just can't imagine why Aunt Grace
would ever think that I wanted you. Why don't you drive
off before that policeman behind us gives you a ticket?'

He shifted the car into drive and pulled out into the
street before checking in his rear view mirror. 'Which
policeman?' he asked as they continued on their way.
'Why Katie Russel, you lied to me just to change the
subject. There was no policeman there!'

She made no answer. He drove slowly, both hands on
the wheel, but the fingers of his right hand were beating a
monotonous tattoo on the leather binding of the steering
aparatus. Nothing further was said until they passed
Temple Hill, where he broke the silence.

'Your stepfather, Katie,' he prodded her. 'Tell me
about him.'

'There's really nothing to tell. He's a fine man. He's
also an outstanding photographer. As far as I can tell he
loves my mother, and she loves him. Don't try to read
anything into it, Harry. When he married my mother I
was just at that foolish state of mind. I went off to the
University, and then, when I came home, things were so
different that—well, I decided to take my camera and
put in my *Wanderjahr*. Probably—well, I worked closely
with my dad. I almost worshipped him. We were closer
than any of the other children. And although I respect
my stepfather, I wasn't quite ready to put him in my
father's place.'

They made the turn at Ernestville, and started to
climb the mountain. 'Besides,' she said pertly, head
bowed, but with a giggly smile on her lips, 'your plan
would never work, you know.'

'What plan?'

'Your plan to marry me and avoid Grandmother.'

'If—' he said. 'If you convince me, it seems pretty
simple.'

'A lot you know,' she giggled. 'Grandma has control of my money. I can't get married without her permission. And *you* would have to ask her!'

'Oh hell,' he groaned. 'I feel like Custer just after he rode up to the Little Big Horn!'

'And that isn't all,' she said relentlessly. 'Don't you ever forget. I've got the powers. I'll give you the biggest case of boils you ever heard of. And not in some convenient place like your arm!'

'Boils, smoils,' he returned, almost absent-mindedly. He turned the Mercedes into the parking lot outside the gates of the house. Only Katie's embarrassed little VW stood there to welcome it. One of his hands turned the key that killed the engine. The other beat another tattoo on the wheel. She sat silently in her seat, leaning forward stiffly.

What in the world can he be scheming now, she asked herself. There's something going on inside that clever head of his. If you marry me? What kind of proposal was that? But if he could only have included one word. One single word. Love!

He came around to her side of the car and opened the door. She swung her legs out on to the ground, refusing his proffered hand, and pulled herself upon on the crutches. He backed away, an unreadable expression on his usually mobile face. Awkwardly at first, she manoeuvred herself on the crutches, across the bridge, up the ramp at the front door, and into the house. He followed some distance behind.

In the hall he caught up with her, and turned her round, with one hand on her shoulder. She shrugged it off. 'You promised. No touching,' she reminded him. He pulled his hand away as if it had been burned.

'Man, you drive a hard bargain, Katie,' he said disconsolately.

'You don't know *hard* yet,' she returned. 'I'm going to take a shower. No, I guess I'd better not. I don't want *this* cast to come to pieces!' She looked down to the lump on her foot and shook her head in disgust.

'You mean you haven't had a shower since you've been here?' he asked.

'Of course not,' she snapped. 'How could I, with that cast on? The best I've been able to do is a hand bath.'

'You go ahead and get ready,' he returned, 'and I'll get you something to take care of the problem.'

She looked at him suspiciously. 'No fooling around?' she queried.

'No. No fooling around,' he laughed. 'Don't you trust me, Katie?'

'About as far as I can throw the kitchen sink,' she retorted.

'Word of honour,' he sighed. 'You go and get ready for that shower, and I'll show you how to do it without getting the cast wet.'

Still not sure whether to believe him or not, she walked slowly down the hall to her room. The crutches had a tendency to slip on the highly polished floor. She limited herself to short steps, and made slow progress. When she was inside her room, with the door closed, her arms reported their tiredness. She collapsed on her bed and slowly stripped, dropping her clothes on the bed beside her. Then she managed the crutches again to reach her heavy towelling robe. The belt of the robe was barely knotted when there was a rap on the door. Without waiting for a response, Harry bustled in.

'You could have waited for me to answer!' she shouted at him.

'Oh my, still that angry? Why should I have waited?'

'Because I was changing my clothes,' she snarled back at him. 'And you knew it. Do you think I'm running some sort of hill-billy peep show?'

'Don't get carried away,' he replied. 'I've seen you before without clothes, if you'll remember.' She *did* remember—that night at the swimming pool, and blushed for her own shame. 'And we don't say *hill-billy* around here,' he continued. 'That's considered a derogatory comment. We say Mountain Men!'

'Oh, all right,' she said, struggling to contain her anger. 'So I was wrong. And I apologise. Now what?'

'Just sit down on this chair,' he ordered. She complied. He unrolled the little bundle in his hand. It turned out to be a small three-ply polyethylene rubbish sack. He opened it up fully, inserted her cast deep inside the bag, then wound the plastic top around her ankle and lower leg, fastening it tightly in place with two heavy rubber bands. Lastly, he fanned out the top of the bag so that it lay smoothly down the back of her leg.

'There you go,' he remarked. She stood up hesitantly and tried to move. 'Want me to help you to the shower,' he asked, with a leer in his voice.

'No, I don't!' she replied, exasperated. She manoeuvred herself out of the room and down to the bathroom. He followed close behind her. At the open door she turned round. 'Why do you do that, Harry?' she asked. 'First you're nice, and then you're indecent. Isn't there any half-way point for you?'

'Not really.' His voice sounded apologetic, but there was a smile lurking at the corners of his mouth. 'I guess I owe it all to my childhood. My mother and father died soon after Amanda was born. I'm an orphan. Does that make you feel more sympathetic?'

'I—I don't think so,' she stammered. 'Is it true?'

'Why, of course it's true,' he answered, all injured innocence. And then he started to laugh. 'It's all true, Katie, but it didn't have any particular effect on either Amanda or me. Aunt Grace raised us, and we could never have asked for a kinder or better parent!'

'Damn you, Harry King,' she shrilled at him. 'That's just what I mean! How in the world is a girl supposed to understand you!' She slammed the bathroom door in his face and leaned against it, shaking. Outside she could hear his laughter fade away as he walked back down the hall.

Her shower was a great success. Someone had left a tall stool in the shower compartment. She dropped her robe, crutched her way into the stall, perched sidewise on the stool, and turned on the water. The first burst of cold water startled her, but the rushing warmth that followed soothed both skin and mind. She used the soap extravagantly in a sensual massage, and then sat under the water's balm for twenty minutes. A niggle of conscience drove her out. She dried herself slowly, and then anointed herself liberally with a bottle of Amanda's Jean Nate after-bath splash.

Katie was fully dressed and drying her hair, when Harry rapped at the door again. This time he waited patiently in the hall until she invited him in. He cracked open the door, stuck his head around the jamb, and announced lunch.

'You made lunch?' she asked, surprised more than she cared to admit.

'Of course I did,' he chuckled. 'Anything's possible.'

'I'll bet it is,' she murmured as she got up and crutched her way across the room.

'What did you say?'

'It's the age of miracles,' she told him blandly, and swung by him on the way to the kitchen. It was more than lunch preparation he had been up to, she saw. A pure white tablecloth covered the usually bare table. Two places had been set, with a full lay-out of silverware, and a vase of plastic flowers served as a centrepiece. He was waiting for some comment.

'Nice. Very nice,' she told him. He held her chair for her, taking her crutches when she was firmly seated, and laying them on the floor at her side.

He served the simple lunch with a flair that brought laugh-crinkles to the corners of her mouth. The soup was quite obviously out of a can, but what kind it had been when it started, she could hardly tell. He had doctored it with all kinds of vegetables and spices, and what might have been a mild vegetable soup had become a Mexican tongue-burner. She managed to down a few spoonsfuls, then pleaded for water.

'Of course. Water!' He jumped up and served her. 'I knew there was something I forgot!' he exclaimed.

'I suspect that's the *only* thing you've overlooked,' she returned, maintaining a firm control over her face muscles. She went back to the soup, and managed to empty the bowl without giving herself away. He hardly noticed the tear in her left eye. It was brought on by spices, not the company.

She declined a second serving, trying to indicate at the same time how nice it all was. But Harry was too full of his own enthusiasm to note. He whipped the soup plates out of the way, and drew out of the oven a tray of melted-cheese open sandwiches.

'The specialty of the house,' he announced. 'They're hot. Have a couple.'

It would have been graceless to decline. She accepted two. He had carefully trimmed off all the crusts, but there was a smoky odour about them. The bottom of each was somewhat more carbonated than one might want. She would not even have looked, had he not been so extremely careful about the way they landed on her plate. Oh well, she told herself. Tonight I'll make a real dinner. Even Ben Franklin couldn't cook!

She waited for the sandwiches to cool, then followed his lead by picking up a quarter in her fingers, and taking a good bite. She knew she was in trouble almost at once. The cheese had a delectably sharp taste, but refused to separate from the bread when she bit down. When she lowered it to the plate, long thin streamers of cheese continued to stick to the portion in her mouth.

'That's lovely, Harry,' she mumbled as she tried to break loose from the threads. 'What kind of cheese did you use?'

'Mozzarella,' he replied. 'Isn't that a great taste?' He was having as much trouble as she was, but it didn't seem to bother him at all.

'It's fine, just fine,' she congratulated him. But she picked up her knife and fork, and very carefully cut the sandwich into bite-sized pieces before she continued.

'That was a fine meal, Harry,' she repeated later as he cleared the table, stuffing the dishes helter-skelter into the dishwasher.

'Well, making a meal is a pretty simple thing,' he flung back over his shoulder. 'Any sensible man could do it if he had to.'

'Oh, of course,' she murmured politely. She got to her feet, excused herself, and crutched her way out into the hall before her temper boiled over. Any man could do it! Meaning, of course, that making a meal might be a problem for a poor simple woman, but *man* need only apply his intellect to the situation, and it would be solved. 'Damn you, Harry King,' she muttered. 'You're not only a chauvinist, but you're too egotistical to know it! Regardless of what your sister says.' Still shaking her head, she meandered over to the door and went outside.

The wind had dropped, and the temperature had risen again. She crutched herself half-way down the path and looked off to the west. Storm clouds were piling up again over Washington County. Big billowing black clouds, occasionally lit by flares of lightning. Her raincoat, she remembered, was still in the back of the VW. Better get it now, she told herself, and moved carefully down the path to the gate. She had been surprised to see that the gate was closed. Now she got an even greater surprise. The gate was locked! A huge padlock, which normally hung on a peg beside the gate, now swung stolidly from the jointure of the heavy chain that sealed the gate shut!

She rattled the gate to be sure. It moved an inch or two on its pinions, but no farther. Why had Harry locked the gate after them? Deep in the pit of her stomach an answer sprang up. She felt a wave of emotion, anger, sweep over her. And then she saw the taxi pulling into the parking lot. Anger turned to elation. She struggled back up the walk to the house. He was standing in the open front door, a bland innocent look on his face.

'Harry, the gate is locked,' she announced through

lips pressed hard together to keep from laughing.

'Perhaps to keep strangers out?' He refused to meet her eye, glancing instead at the beginnings of the storm massing above them, looking very much like a boy caught with his hand in the biscuit tin.

'Mr King,' she said flatly. 'For once, the plain unvarnished truth. Why is the gate locked?'

'Okay, Katie,' he said sombrely, still fidgeting. 'The truth. The gate is locked, and it's going to stay locked until you and I have had a long talk.'

'So,' she hissed at him, 'I'm a prisoner? Your prisoner?'

'Now, Katie,' he pleaded, 'it's not that bad. I locked it as well to keep people out, you know. It gives us a chance to know each other, without all the interruptions that go on around this crazy place.'

'Well, I think you'd better give it a second thought,' she said, turning her back on him. Not just to see the tall thin figure of the woman stalking over the bridge, but also to keep herself from giggling in his face.

'Why should I?' he gruffed. 'I think it's a grand plan.'

'Your grand plan has just come unstuck,' she returned, unable to restrain herself any further. 'You have a visitor.'

'Don't worry,' he growled, peering down at the gate. 'Some old biddy. She can't get in.'

'She'd better, Harry King, if you know what's good for you.'

'What the devil are you talking about? Do you know her?'

'I wouldn't be surprised.' And the giggles broke loose. She wheeled around to look up into his startled beet-red face. 'You've struck out at last, mountain man. That's the Seventh Cavalry coming to the rescue. Or, to be more precise, that old biddy down there is my Grandmother Russel!'

CHAPTER ELEVEN

THE kitchen seemed very crowded, although there were only three of them there. Grandma Russel sat down abruptly in the biggest of the kitchen chairs and sighed. 'At my age,' she mourned, 'to have to shorten my Miami vacation and come climbing around these stupid mountains. You'd have a fine lot of land here, sonny, if only it wasn't piled up and down. You couldn't pull it out and stretch it flat?'

'We—uh,' he stammered. Katie moved around the table for a better view, a wide grin on her face. She had stood to attention during Grandmother's interrogations more times than one. Mr Harry King was about to have his head handed to him, piece by piece.

'We people sort of like it this way,' he finally got out. The matriarch looked around at her grandchild. 'Somebody—some Aunt Grace—?'

'Yes, Aunt Grace,' Katie confirmed.

'Aunt Grace called your mother yesterday, and gave her some mishmash about you had a broken foot, and would be all alone up here at the mercy of some man. You know how your mother dithers. Rather than tell her husband, she called me in Florida. And here I am. Is this the man?'

It hardly seemed worth pointing out that there was only one man on view. 'Don't like red-headed men,' Grandma continued. 'Never did. Devious, they are. What's your name, sonny?'

'Er—King,' he gulped. 'Harry King. You look a great deal like your—like Katie, ma'am.'

'Typical,' the old lady snapped. '*I* came first. Seventy-one years ago, to be exact. *She* looks somewhat like me. Wear the same size clothes, we do. Or at least we did.

Katie, you look like a scarecrow. They've not been feeding you?'

Before Katie could whip up a reasonable answer there came a pounding on the door. 'Better tend to your door,' Grandma said grandly. 'I don't answer doors, and my poor Katherine has a broken foot.'

Harry had been just ready to sit down, and actually had his knees half-flexed when the first knock came. At the second pounding, a look of confusion on his face, he went down the hall to the front door. When he came back there was a small white-haired man with him.

'She said you would pay, Mr King,' the man said. 'All the way from the airport at Johnson City, mind you. I was goin' to turn her down, you know, and I was all set to say so, when the first thing I know we was driving down the highway. She said you was going to pay.'

'I'll pay, I'll pay,' Harry groaned. He reached into his pocket and pulled out a roll of bills. His eyes blinked when the taxi driver told him the amount, but he peeled off the required payment.

'Katherine,' Grandma snapped. 'No hospitality? No coffee? Don't tell me you can't get around at all?'

'I—I can get around,' she returned, blushing. 'Coffee?'

'You too, Mr—?' Grandma turned to the cab driver. 'We can't have you driving off in a storm without at least a cup of coffee.'

'Lauder, ma'am,' the driver said. 'Frank Lauder. And I'd be pleased to have a cup of coffee.' He took the chair she motioned him into. Harry stood with his mouth half-open. At Katie's giggle he snapped it shut and glared at her.

She bustled as best she could, with her mind not at all on what her hands were doing. He looks as if he's just been assaulted by half the army, she told herself. And if Grandma keeps it up she'll cut him down from six foot four to two foot nothing. And why does that bother me? Because—because I don't want that to happen, that's why! Because underneath that disguise of his he's really such a nice guy—and I imagine that I—that any girl—could fall in love with him. Even Eloise. His ego is important to him—and he's important to me! She stopped what she was doing and sent a pleading look at her grandmother. And got back a non-committal smile.

The men carried the coffee mugs to the table. The cab driver treasured his between his hands, warming them. Grandma Russel sipped delicately at hers. Harry gulped, and immediately sputtered as the hot liquid brought him to his senses. Katie barely touched hers, but kept her eyes on their faces.

'So now,' Grandma said. 'What do you do for a living, Mr King?'

The cab driver leaned interestedly forward. 'I'm an inventor,' Harry returned. 'I invent things. You know.'

'Oh yes. I know.' Grandmother was being her sweetest. 'We have a couple of men like you in my home town, so you don't have a steady job?'

'Well—' Harry stuttered. 'I work every day, if that's what you mean.'

'He works very hard,' Katie interjected. He looked up and smiled across the table at her, a special *thank you* smile.

'Of course,' Grandma continued in her musing, 'some men are like that. They never seem to realise that it's less work to have a job than to keep avoiding one. Never *ever* had a steady job, have you?'

His face was stone-carved. The fingers of one hand drummed on the table top. Lord, he's mad, Katie told herself. Like a volcano. Any minute now, his top is going to blow off, and there'll be lava all over the kitchen! But then, very slowly, it was no longer anger that formed facial contours. His lip twitched, and a worried expression flashed at her out of those deep blue eyes. As if he wanted to impress someone.

'As a matter of fact,' he said, 'I had a job when I went to college. I worked as a waiter. Does that count?'

'A college man? Well, that wouldn't be held against you. Not ordinarily. Enjoy the hard work, did you?'

'I can't say that I did, now that I think back on it. Inventing seems to be a much better way of life. Oh, I spent some time in the army, too. In Vietnam. Does that count?'

'That's something. Nothing I like better than a boy who serves his country. Work your way up, did you?'

'I—well—all the way to Private First Class.'

'Ain't wrong to be ambitious,' Mr Lauder commented. 'And there's plenty of jobs down in the valley. White Cabs could use two more drivers, tell the truth. You drive?'

'Can't say that I do,' Harry reflected grimly. 'Besides, I couldn't stand all those talkative customers.'

'Ah, there's always that,' the driver responded sadly. 'Talk, talk, talk. Makes a man old before his time.'

'Don't you have to get back to work, Mr Lauder?' Katie felt compelled to get him out of the way. The cabbie took the hint. He took one last swig at the coffee, wiped his mouth with the back of his hand, and got up. Harry escorted him to the door. Sitting in the kitchen, the two women could hear his high-pitched laugh as he had a parting word.

'You be sure to let me know how it all turns out!'

'Yes, I'll do that,' rolled Harry's deep bass. 'Nice to have interested neighbours—I think.'

Katie looked over at her grandmother and caught the solemn look playing at the corners of her mouth. 'I came, young lady, because it seems to me you're in a terrible fix.'

'I don't know what you mean, Grandma.'

'I do believe you're a little slow,' the old lady laughed. 'You don't have the slightest idea what he's about, do you? You know, there's someone he reminds me of—I can't seem to put my mind to it exactly. Oh well, it'll come to me. Has he asked you to marry him?'

'Yes—well—' Katie sighed. 'He seems to have this

thing against marriage. He wouldn't mind a live-in girlfriend, but the ring bit, that seems to put him off.'

'I know. I've seen a passel of them before.' Grandmother shifted herself around in the chair to get comfortable. 'Lost too much flesh myself, I have,' she grumbled. 'Bones stick out everywhere. When sittin' ain't fun, lovin' ain't either. Your grandfather used to say that. Well, don't worry your head about him, girl. He's no prize. We'll start off to Ohio tomorrow morning. Everybody is expecting you. Marion is head over tea-cup about the wedding. Like this man, do you?'

'I—I'm not sure,' Katie sighed. 'Well, I'm sure about me, but not about him. I don't think—'

'That's the trouble with your generation,' her grandmother interrupted. 'Too much thinking. You need to let yourself go!'

'Grandma!' Any further conversation was cut off, as Harry came back into the room.

'Now, where were we,' he asked, rubbing his hands together in that patented shuffle that meant he was spoiling for a fight. I should have warned Grandma, Katie thought. He's dangerous when he's like that. But then so is Grandma!

'Employment,' Harry offered.

'Which you don't have much of,' Grandma snapped. 'Can't hardly afford to keep yourself, never mind a wife. Huh!'

'I was thinking about getting work,' he offered, 'and then I thought to marry money. Can I offer you supper?'

'Oh? You cook do you?' Oh no, not that, Katie screamed to herself. Not that. He's a major catastrophe in the kitchen. A threat to life and limb!

'I could cook something,' she offered. Anything to keep him out of the kitchen. Anything! She struggled up on to her crutches and started to forage for a meal.

'Too bad about your foot, Katie,' her grandmother mused from her throne at the kitchen table. 'However did it happen, Mr King?'

He was caught off-stride again, and the colours flushed through his tan. 'I—there was this accident.'

'Oh? Tell me about it.'

'Grandmother, do you like—' she interjected, trying to change the subject, but the matriarch had the bit in her teeth, and was running.

'You know what I like,' the old lady snapped. 'Just get about your business while I get about mine. You were saying, Mr King?'

'It was—well—Katie wanted to get some pictures from the top of the mountain. So I took her up there, and she was taking some snaps, and this rock fell and hit her foot.'

'How inconvenient. The rock had been poised there since Creation Day, just waiting for Katherine to come along?'

'To tell the truth, I was—'

'Aha! You were. You dropped the rock on her foot, did you?'

'Damnit, yes! I dropped the rock on her foot! And there's no use you trying to give me a guilt-trip. I've been on one ever since the accident. Yes. I dropped a rock on Katherine's foot, and broke it—the foot, I mean.'

'I know what you mean. And you needn't curse at me, young man. And then wasn't there something about pushing her into the swimming pool?'

'No, Grandmother!' Katie was unable to hold back the wail of anguish. Nor was she so stupid that she didn't know what it revealed of her own feelings. 'Not Harry. He didn't push me in. He jumped in after me and saved my life.'

'That's something to his credit,' the old woman commented. 'I was beginning to think it was all coming out on the wrong side of the ledger. Now then, young man, show me around this place while Katie fixes a meal. Worst thing in the world, having a man hanging around the kitchen.'

The two of them went off together. Katie made her

initial preparations, and then sat down at the table to console herself. Harry's plan had certainly been derailed, but who would ever think that Grandma would come all the way up here? It was hard not to giggle, and yet—she didn't feel particularly happy about it at all. It had almost seemed when Eloise went on her way, that the road to happiness was completely clear. Then we meet this other roadblock—'I'm not the marrying kind!' Well, *I* am, Katie mumbled as she got up to finish the potato salad. *I* am. He wants me, and the only way he's going to get me is—my bedroom is just down the hall from the altar! That's what Aunt Becky said all the time—but she's still a spinster! Oh Lord. Maybe I don't feel all that strong about the formalities. Maybe I just want him myself—just that, with no trimmings!

Their return startled her. She glanced at the clock. It had been a good two hours she had sat there mooning, unable to come to any real decision, but—just slightly— wishing that Harry's plan might have worked! She climbed up on to her crutches and started the steaks.

'We'll stay the night, and tomorrow we'll leave for Ohio.' Grandmother was sitting in Aunt Grace's rocking chair in the living room, after having expounded at length on how good a cook Katie was, and how wonderful with children. Katie sat on the forward edge of her straight-backed chair, trying to find some way to cut off the excess of remembrances. Harry relaxed on the couch, sprawled out in a half-sitting position, and eating it all up. Until Grandmother, watching his face, threw him another curveball.

'There's nothing wrong with toy-making,' she said. 'You've got some fine toys in the cellar there. Lots of money to be made in toys these days. The market is always ready for something new. But you would have to stick to it, you understand, if you expect to be able to support a family. Did I mention, Katie, that Harry wants a large family? Good thing, that, if you can afford it.'

Katie's face turned instant scarlet. What sort of an

answer can you give to a statement like that? She fidgeted in her chair, tucking at her skirt, crossing her feet at the ankles, twisted both hands together in her lap.

'Or is it, Mr King,' her grandmother continued speculatively, 'that you're after the poor girl's money?'

'Well really—' Katie sputtered. 'Really, Grandmother. There isn't all that much to begin with! What a thing to say!'

'Best said than left behind the door,' her grandmother offered. 'Or—can it be that you're after *my* money, sonny?'

From across the room Katie could see him turn red, and then purple, as he made a massive effort to stave off comment. She scrambled up from her chair and took two faltering steps in his direction, but he held up a hand, palm open, in the age-old stop signal. She sighed, and backed up to her chair again.

'No, ma'am,' he said through clenched teeth. 'I never did know that you had any money, and if you did, no idea that Katie might get it. Please believe me, Mrs Russel. I have no designs on your grandchild's money.'

'Huh!' the old lady snorted. 'That's as may be, young man. But you've got designs on *something*. Lucky that I arrived today. Mind you, I have a barrel full of grandchildren, but Katie is the pick of the litter. I think well of my Katherine. And you can rest assured, when my time comes, Katie will get all my money. Every cent. Now then, it's growing late, and I've been up since early dawn this day. And at my age, I need my sleep.'

Katie got up as her grandmother did. 'I'll go with you to your room,' she suggested. The old lady had been assigned Eloise's old room, and the stairs were steep. Katie hobbled out as far as the hallway, where the old lady seized her arm.

'He's an arrogant, domineering man,' her grandmother hissed in her ear. 'If you give him an inch you'll never own your own life again. With that sort of man you fight all the time, rear up on your hind legs and let him know who's boss!'

'You don't like him, Grandma?' She felt an immediate sense of sorrow. That *some* people might not like Harry, this she could believe. But not Grandmother. They were too much alike, this old lady and herself. And it strangely hurt to think—

'Well, now,' her grandmother added gruffly, 'I don't need your help out here, little miss. Dry up those tears. Go back and make your goodbyes. We won't have much time in the morning.' Her grandmother chucked her under the chin and steamed off for the stairs.

Harry was standing in the middle of the room, his eyes glued to the door, when she came back. He relaxed when he saw she was alone, and a smile flashed across his face, settling down into that wide grin. What was it that his sister had said? He uses that grin to hide behind when he's uncertain? Huh!

'A whirlwind of a woman,' he said. She watched his eyes. It *did* seem that only his teeth were grinning, as if there was a flood of doubt in his eyes. 'Is that how you're going to look in sixty years, Katie?'

'I don't know,' she said quietly, still watching him. 'I can hardly manage until tomorrow. Sixty years is too much of a guess.'

'But for sure you'll look like her, Katie.'

'I—I suppose,' she offered hesitantly. 'I'm tired. I think I'd better go to bed.'

'And all alone, too,' he sighed. 'What a shame. I had the best plan in the world. It *would* have worked!' He seemed to be confiding in himself.

'Maybe,' she whispered. 'Maybe. I—good night, Mr King.'

He moved close enough to engage both her hands in his. 'Don't rush off with the cold shoulder, Miss Russel,' he gritted. 'Your grandmother upset all my plans. But I still want you, Katie Russel. Why don't we get married?'

I want you, Katie Russel. There it was, still the same. I

want you. She snatched her hands back, almost losing her balance on her crutches. 'What's the matter,' she snarled. 'Has my grandmother convinced you I'm worth having? All of a sudden you've become the marrying kind?'

'Not all of a sudden,' he snapped back. 'It's been a long, losing battle. And yes, your grandmother convinced me. Just the thought of having someone like her around to argue with for sixty years, that's great promise. Well?'

She shuffled around clumsily on her sticks, and started out the door. 'No answer?' he called to her retreating back.

Yes, her mind screamed into a blocked throat. Yes. Just tell me that you love me. But he had nothing more to say, and she paused not a second in her flight to her room.

Damn the man, she told herself as she dropped face down on to her bed. Damn the man! Whatever happened to moonlight and roses, love and laughter, and live happily ever after? So he's a proud Mountain Man. Does that guarantee that he has ice water in his veins? It's a lovely day, and I don't have anything else to do, so why don't we get married? And if we do, I'll keep you locked up in a cage, and perhaps let you out on alternate Sunday afternoons. Damn the man!

She beat down both her pillows in an attempt to scatter her frustrations. Mountain Man! Too bad the Indians didn't scalp them all the very first time they set foot on this side of the mountains! Come marry me and be my love, and we shall love forever! She halted her tantrum and lay silently savouring that last thought. Come marry me and be my love. If only we could. If only he would say something like that! What would Grandmother say? What would—and too tired from all the wild turmoil of the day, she dropped off into a deep sleep.

'Katherine? Katherine!' A gentle hand rested lightly

on her shoulder. She scrambled back to awareness.

'Grandmother?'

'Yes, child. It's almost ten, and there's another storm brewing. Up you come. We're going home today.'

'Today? Must we?'

'Yes, of course we must. Where's your faith, child, do you think he's the only man left in the world?'

'No—I—'

'Then up you get. We'll be in the kitchen.'

'We?'

'Mr King is making us breakfast.'

'Oh, God no, that's a disaster in the making.'

'Let him struggle, girl. He's got a lot of thinking to do yet. It's obvious that he didn't sleep a wink last night. Neither did you, did you? Into the bathroom then, and come along.'

She still had sand in her eyes when she crutched her way out to the kitchen. A new tablecloth, cerulean blue, with white flowers embroidered in the corners, had replaced the utilitarian white of the past few days. She adjusted herself to the chair without looking at him, then sat up primly, with back straight and hands in her lap.

He watched her from dark eyes. She could see the tired expression, the slight tic under his eye. He brought a plate for her, another for her grandmother. She looked down at the watery mess, and then glanced sideways. Her grandmother was hacking away at the scrambled eggs as if they were a gift from the gods. There was a warning gleam in the old woman's eyes. Katie dug in, trying to look enthusiastic. The toast was too much. It looked like a scorched timber from a barn fire. Surreptitiously she crumbled it up and brushed the pieces into her napkin.

'It's a terrible day for travel,' he offered. He seemed to be having trouble drinking his coffee. And that's something, Katie told herself. He needs a cook. He couldn't survive on his own without one. But the trouble is that there have been too many women in the past willing to pander to him!

'Oh, I don't know,' Grandmother Russel returned. 'With the rain and all it will be cool. Katherine is a superb chauffeur. We'll drive as far as the airport, leave the car there, and—just think—Marion will be married in just three more days!'

'Yes, wonderful,' Katie sighed. Why do I have to think about Marion getting married? Why not me? Maybe he won't let us go! That would be a terribly arrogant thing to do. I wish he would.

'But Katie hasn't driven in a long time,' he protested. She could hear a note of desperation in his voice. 'And with that cast—'

'Not to worry,' Grandmother chided him. 'We'll do just fine. Finished with your coffee, love?'

'I—yes. Are we—shall we go right away?'

'Right away, my dear. Thank you for everything, Mr King.'

'For what?' he asked glumly.

'Why for taking care of my favourite grandchild all this time. And I do wish you well for the future. Oh, Katie, I forgot to mention—' this in a somewhat louder voice as the two women made their way out the door— 'Teddy Malson is back in town and asking for you. You remember Teddy?' And so into Katie's bedroom.

'It won't take me a minute to pack,' the younger woman sighed. 'I did most of it yesterday. Why would you bring up Teddy Malson? I don't understand, Grandma. We split up five years ago.'

'And probably the smartest thing you ever did,' the old lady assured her. 'Now get a move on, girl.'

'It's all turning into some kind of second-class melo-drama,' Katie sighed. She took a few minutes to splash cold water on her face again, and started for the door, feeling as miserable as a woman can get. He didn't even come to the door. She slammed it behind her and started down the path. Just across the bridge was her little

Volkswagen, all re-built, re-tested, and returned. The key was in her purse, and the gate was open.

A crash of thunder, following hard on a flash of lightning, startled her. She jumped a pace or two, and almost fell over as one of her crutches slipped off the edge of the flagstones into the soft earth of the flower bed. The lightning had struck one of a clump of tall, thin ash trees across the highway above them. She watched in fascination as the tree split right down the middle and collapsed across the road. And then the rain came.

'Hurry up before we drown,' her grandmother yelled. The older woman, going ahead, had already reached the little car and slipped inside. Katie put her head down and doggedly crutched her way down the path. In the middle of the bridge, heedless of the downpour, she stopped to look down at the broiling creek, now almost half-way up it's gorge. I think I'll change your name to Rubicon, she mused. Some of the water running down her face was salty. She adjusted her crutches under her arms and made her way to the little car.

The door on the driver's side was stuck. She had to wipe an eye clear before she could open it. She slumped into the seat, ducking automatically to avoid bumping her head. Her foot came into the car with ease, but the tiny clutch pedal was difficult to find with her cast. She practised movement of clutch and brake for several tries, telling herself how properly conservative it was. But her eyes were on the house. Once before she had gone through this same drill, and he had come after her. But not this time.

I'll give him another minute, she whispered to herself. But when that minute had passed and nothing had happened, she recognised total defeat. She inserted the key, and turned on the ignition. The engine at the back caught on the first rotation, and began a pleasant rumble. Any other time you would have stalled, she screamed silently. 'Is everything against me?'

Her grandmother's hand came over on top of her own.

'Everything happens in its own good time,' she said. 'Don't cry.' Another crash of thunder seemed to punctuate her statement, but Katie found cold comfort in it all.

She fumbled again with gear stick and clutch, and backed slowly out of the parking place. Ever so slowly, watching the house all the time, eyes filled with desperation, heart with despondency. 'Oh God,' she moaned, 'I'm going to be an old maid!'

'Nonsense,' her grandmother snapped. 'Show a little pride. And don't drive too fast!'

Katie smashed the gear stick forward, ignoring the grinding of metal, and raised her left foot. The old car jerked forward, then began a steady crawl in first gear down the mountain. As she went around the curve where Cove Road joined the main highway, the house disappeared from sight.

Warily she tried to shift into another range, but her cast was too cumbersome. 'To hell with it,' she snarled at the world, and continued down the mountain at low speed. Her grandmother shifted and squirmed to find a comfortable spot in the seat, and said nothing. The rain came down harder. Huge globules of water splashed over the windscreen and rendered the wipers useless. Even the world is crying, she told herself. Whoever would think that I'd finish my trip in such a mess as this?

She hunched forward in her seat, pressing her breasts hard against the metal ring of the steering wheel, peering forward with maximum concentration. But another lightning flash dead ahead of her frightened her more than she could believe possible. An old hickory tree, stripped by the blast, teetered in the air, wavered, and fell backwards into the brush behind it. Thunder rolled. And a strange sound was filling the car. Her grandmother was humming a tune, some old-fashioned ditty.

It was the last straw. Her eyes blinded by tears, raw sobs tearing at her throat, she tried to steer the wobbling car to the side of the road, only to find herself on the soft shoulder. She slammed on the brakes, and everything after that was like a slow-motion movie. The car, which had been barely making eight miles an hour, slid on the soft wet dirt, and stopped with the right front wheel out over the drainage ditch beside the road. The vehicle rocked back and forth gently, aided by gusts of wind. And then, like an old dowager measuring a seat on a bus, it slid over the edge and into the ditch.

'And that,' her grandmother said in a very disgusted tone, 'ought to just about do it!'

Katie sat behind the wheel, stunned. Neither of them was hurt in the least. The descent had been too slow for that. The car was in good condition. The motor purred behind her, the windscreen wipers clicked busily along, and the rain was shut out. The only small problem was that the car was nose-down in a foot of running water, with its tail sticking up at such an angle that the back wheels were off the ground. They'll put up a tablet for me, she told herself hysterically, 'Katherine Russel, Moron'. Right here at this bend in the road, no doubt. I have to get help. I *have* to! Grandma can't stay out for long in this sort of weather!

She shut off the motor, patted the seat of the old car affectionately, and pushed open the door on her side. 'I'll walk on down the mountain,' she yelled over the noise of the rain. 'There is bound to be someone to help. The car is perfectly safe, so you just stay inside here.'

'Of course, love. You can't really fight fate. Off you go!'

For just a split second that strange sound in her grandmother's voice nagged at Katie's sub-conscious, but she shook it off. She pushed herself out into the rain, feeling as if she should shake her fist at the wild sky. Her crutches came out from behind the front seat. She slammed the door behind her, waved an encouragement to her grandmother, and started down the empty highway.

The shoulder of the road made hard going. The crutches jammed themselves down into the mud two or

three inches each time she moved them, and came out
with a slow plop as suction locked on to the hard rubber
pads at their ends. It took her some time to manoeuvre
over on to the tarmac. She stopped to catch her breath.
Her clothes were soaked. The little knit sweater clung to
her like a second skin, and her wet hair seemed to weigh
a ton.

She swung herself around, wiped a little of the cascade
out of her eyes, and hobbled down the mountain. What a
damnable joke, she told herself. Me! I'm not fit to be let
out without a keeper. And look at my new cast. She held
it out slightly in front of her. Water was running down
her leg and into the cast like a freshet. Lord, the doctor
will scream when he sees this, she giggled hysterically.

She plucked up her courage and struggled on, trying
to get some rhythm into her movements. 'Katie Russel,
dummy, dummy,' she started to chant, and the movement became easier. She was already out of sight of the
Volkswagen, and so entirely wrapped up in the movement of her feet, the advancement of the crutches and
the hypnotic sound of the chant, that she hardly heard
when the big Mercedes whispered up behind her,
passed, and slowed to a dead stop directly in her path.

'My God, Katie,' he roared as he snatched her up in
his arms. The crutches fell to the ground, and one of
them slipped into the ditch.

'I need them,' she screamed at him, beating on his
shoulders with her clenched fists. 'I have to get help for
Grandma.'

'Your grandmother is in the back seat of my car,' he
roared back at her. She ducked, as if expecting a physical
assault. 'Girl, you'd better duck,' he yelled. 'You're not
fit to be out without a keeper. I swear I don't know which
one of us is the most stupid. Me, for wasting all these
weeks, or you, running at the first chance you got! And
you *are* going to marry me, you little witch!'

'I am not,' she screamed back at him. 'What did you
call me?'

'Witch,' he reiterated. 'Witch. A totally brainless witch!'

'Don't you dare say that,' she roared back at him. 'You're not all that bright either. If you were, we wouldn't be out here in the rain catching pneumonia!'

'Ahhhhhhhhrrrrrrh!' The noise sounded as if he were strangling. 'Rain or no rain,' he yelled in fury, 'this is going to be settled right now. And if you think I'm going to have it all out in front of that—that grandmother of yours, you're crazy!'

'You don't like my grandmother?' She brushed her sopping hair aside and looked up into his troubled eyes.

'That's got nothing to do with it,' he snarled. '*She* doesn't like me! Why is that, Katherine?'

'I don't know,' she snapped back at him. 'Grandma likes most people. Most nice people, that is.'

'Don't be so smart,' he returned. 'I'm as nice as anyone can be. Anybody will tell you that. My God, look at you. You're soaked to the skin. What an idiotic thing that was, to drive your car into the ditch.'

His disdain was enough to trigger off one last burst of defiance. 'Yes, and I did it all on purpose,' she shouted at him. 'And I'm not going to marry you. You hear!'

'Everybody between here and Tilson's Mill can hear,' he retorted. But his tone had shifted. There was a question behind his every word. He took a deep breath, and continued at a normal conversational level. 'Now, let's get this settled. I couldn't tell you how I felt until I had Eloise settled. I had promises to keep. Now all that's behind me—and so is my idiotic notion about marriage. I've chased you long enough. If I didn't love you so much I would have put poison in your soup. You are a beautiful, headstrong girl, and I'm going to take care of you.'

She ducked her head away from him. 'You might be right,' she muttered. If I didn't love you so much? Her mind whirled, broke loose from reason, and left her speechless. The rain had penetrated all her clothes now.

She could feel its cold fingers running down over her breasts and stomach.

'Well, that's a start,' he snapped. 'Now listen. I talked to your mother on the telephone last night. She thinks we should get married. My Aunt Grace wants you to marry me. She thinks it would be my salvation. And *I* want you to marry me. Who the devil is Teddy Whatchamacallit?'

'Teddy?' She was just coming back down to earth. 'Teddy Malson. We were engaged once, a long time ago. He was worse than you are!'

'What! Another arrogant, dominating male?'

'No,' she sighed. 'A wishy-washy man who couldn't make up his mind to anything. Grandmother didn't like him, either. Why can't we get in out of the rain? I'm getting—' A shiver ran up and down her spine, replacing all the words.

'Damnit! What kind of a fool am I?' He swept her clear of her feet and carried her the short distance to the car. It took but a moment for him to come round, start the engine, and turn on the blessed heater.

'Grandmother?' She twisted round to peer into the back seat. 'Are you all right?'

The old lady was sitting primly in the middle of the wide seat, a folded newspaper in her hands. 'I'm fine, Katherine,' she said softly. 'Pretty silly of you to stand out there in the rain, wasn't it? Have a lot to talk about, did you?'

Katie relaxed in the warmth, and then her mind came suddenly awake. He had said, out there in the rain— what, exactly? She turned to look at him. He was staring straight ahead, brooding over the steering wheel.

'What you said out there—' she stammered. 'You said—'

'I said that I love you, and I want to marry you. Has that finally sunk in?'

'You don't have to be so surly about it,' she told him soberly. 'You don't leave any room for what *I* want.

You—would you run that whole conversation by me again?'

'I love you,' he said. 'All the sensible people around you know what's good for you. All you have to do is what you're told!' He leaned over her, a large brooding shadow, water dripping down from his thatch of hair and falling off his nose. She shivered as he pulled a blanket from the back seat and wrapped it around her.

'You love me?' she queried weakly.

'Of course I do,' he muttered, pulling her into his arms. 'Why do you suppose I kept making all those ridiculous excuses to kiss you? Damn, this is like making love to a mermaid. There isn't a dry spot on you anywhere. Where was I? Yes. All you have to do is to relax and do what I tell you. We'll go down to Johnson City and we'll catch one of those big flying birds, and we'll go to Marion's wedding. And yours. Now, all you need to do is to keep practising "I will" over and over again. That's not too hard, even for a photographer, is it?' And there it was again. Strong words, and behind it the little quaver of a man who hoped it could all be true if only he kept saying it often enough.

She heard the words, and the undertones, and smiled secretly. 'But we can't crash Marion's wedding like that,' she said. 'I don't—Marion will be mad at me—Mama won't—I don't have—'

'Don't fluster, love,' he said softly. 'I have already asked your mother and your sister. They both approve.'

A hand came over the seat to rest on her shoulder. A thin blue-veined hand, full of love. 'I've just remembered who he reminds me of,' her grandmother said from the back of the car. 'A thoroughly detestable arrogant man. Your Grandfather Russel!'

'I—Grandpa? But you married him, love?'

'Yes I did, didn't I? And we spent half a century together. I can't really remember which was better—the arguments we had, or the times we spent making up after them! Bad times and good, it was all so wonderful. But

Lord he was an arrogant opinionated man!'

'Then—you think I should—'

'Do what your heart tells you,' her grandmother said softly.

She could almost see him deflate as a huge sigh ran out of him. His hand moved towards the automatic drive, and then stopped. 'What's wrong now?'

'I'm crying, that's what. Can't a girl cry if she wants to? What kind of a place is this to propose to somebody? Whatever happened to roses and love me forever?'

'I think I've already loved you for half of forever.' His voice was a soft caress, a breath of warmth for the heart. 'And I'll get you a rose when we go through Erwin. Right after I buy you a handkerchief. Or maybe a towel. Say, you are a mess, aren't you?'

'Well thank you. Your friends speak well of you too!'

'Now that's enough of that,' he said quietly. 'Just because I'm sweet-talking you doesn't mean that you can wear the pants in our family. Just come along quietly and do what I tell you. And after we get married your grandmother is not going to come within a hundred miles of you without my express invitation.' There was a warm chuckle from the rear seat, and the rattle of a newspaper as Grandmother Russel buried her head in the pages.

His arms came over and tightened around her, leaving spots of warmth where they caressed the wet silk of her blouse. She lifted her face up to him, and watched as the world was blotted out. His lips touched hers, shutting out sky and air and sound, turning on all her alarms, sparking all her bodily responses. When he reluctantly broke contact she was shaken, breathless, but not totally submissive.

'Did you like that?' he enquired casually. Or at least it sounded casual, as always. But now, measured by a heart full of love, she could hear all the doubts behind it.

'Yes,' she answered quietly. 'I liked that very much.'

'Then you *are* going to marry me!' There was the

undertone of triumph behind the words. She tucked her face into his broad chest, squirming against him for the comfort that she knew was there. It really isn't surrender, she told her own proud heart. It's just a sort of—well—amalgamation.

'I'm going to do what I'm told,' she whispered into his second shirt button. His whole body seemed to relax in another massive sigh of relief.

'Can we really go now?' Grandmother Russel asked from the back seat. 'I've a plane to catch, and this newspaper is a week old.'

CHAPTER TWELVE

A YEAR rolled by, and half again. Spring rested lightly on the Great Smokey's enblazoned flanks. The scarlet of the flame azaleas had fled down the wind, and the blue, white and red of the mountain laurel and the rhododendron drew the tourists in their thousands to see the mountains sparkle.

Katie King stretched herself out on the lounger by the pool, patting the flatness of her stomach. Across the table from her Mary worked industriously at the keyboard of the word processor, following Aunt Grace's dictation. The young girl looked fresh and happy, her foot almost corrected, as she nibbled her lip and touched the keys. When Aunt Grace came to the end of her reading they all dropped back in their chairs, laughing.

'Katie,' the girl cried, 'I'll never be able to thank you for this wonderful training.'

'Don't thank me, Mary. Thank Harry. Remember what Oz said. You need the information *and* the diploma!'

'Just what did Harry do, dear?' Aunt Grace asked. 'By the time I heard about it I was too confused to think straight.'

Katie laughed so loudly that a small wail of disgust came from the little cradle beside her. She rocked it with her foot. 'Mary really needed a college degree,' she explained. 'So Harry organised and incorporated Bald Mountain Business College. Harry is the Dean, I'm the instructor, and Mary is the only pupil. I suspect that before anyone comes around to question we will have graduated our entire class. Lord, that man has gall!'

'Looks like he's got more than gall,' Aunt Grace said proudly. 'Look at him. He's got what we used to call a self-satisfied smirk on his face!'

Katie twisted in her chair to watch her husband amble across the grass towards them. Even after a year and a half, she caught her breath at the sight of him. Like a big ambling red-headed cuddly bear, she told herself, and giggled at her own temerity. My lord and master. I ought to kiss his foot! Suiting words to actions, she darted up from the chair, took the few steps towards him, and dropped to the ground. He came to a rumbling halt, eyes sparkling with glee as she dropped a kiss on the toe showing through his open sandals.

'Now that's the way a man ought to be greeted,' he declared, as he pulled her up to her feet.

'I would have done it sooner, but I couldn't bend over,' she laughed.

'Are you taking notes, Mary,' he called. 'Humble. Submissive, obedient. That's the way to hold a man.'

'Wait 'll I get you in bed tonight,' Katie threatened in his ear. 'We'll see how fast I can cut Superman down to the mortal ranks.'

'None of that,' he remonstrated. 'There are minors present.'

'I don't care what you say,' Mary chimed in. 'She's got the powers. And that's what I'm fixing to study. *That*'s the way to hold a man!'

Harry set Katie down on her lounger, and walked around so he could see his sleeping son right side up. He stood fixed in position, as if a move would wake the child. His teeth were nibbling at his lower lip. He had the look of—reverence—on his face. He sat down on the bottom half of Katie's chair. 'I almost forgot,' he said. 'I got a letter from Eloise. She's expecting.'

'Somebody slipped up there,' Aunt Grace chuckled. 'C'mon, Mary, help me back to the house. Your mother and I are going to make jelly this afternoon.'

Katie leaned back in the chair and watched them go.

'She's slowing down,' she remarked. 'But her arthritis doesn't seem to bother her any more.'

'Come off it,' Harry laughed. 'You know darn well she never had arthritis. It was all part of a plot to trap me.'

'Poor boy,' she commiserated. 'Trapped by women's wiles!' She stretched out, so that her foot rested in his lap. He put one hand over it, and began to draw circles on the bare flesh. A languid feeling came over Katie, and her eyes focused on far distant things.

'What are you thinking about?'

'The wedding. How we got to Humbersville still in all those wet rumpled clothes. And I barely had time for a shower before I was crammed into Grandma's wedding dress. I thought she'd have a fit when she saw how the bodice fitted. She wanted me to stuff it with Kleenex— can you imagine that? And then, when I was ready to go down the aisle my brother had to drop everything and go rent me another pair of crutches.'

'You could have been married in the wheelchair,' he reminded her. 'I already had that.'

'If you thought I was going to marry you sitting down, you had another think coming,' she teased him. 'You had enough advantages over me without that!'

'You talk about advantages,' he snorted. 'How about me? All alone at the reception. Every time I turned around some great big hulking relative of yours would come up to me, stuff his hands in his pockets, and say "So you're the Mountain Man, huh?"—as if I had some kind of infectious disease!'

'But all the girls thought you were marvellous, dear,' she soothed him. 'My niece Becky said she was sorry you married me, because when she got to be fifteen she'd like to marry you herself. That makes you feel better?'

'Yes, it does, Katie. *You* make me feel better. I'm much more secure in these valleys with you at my side.'

'Well, you shouldn't be,' she laughed. 'Little Harry is Grandma's first step in the plan to capture the valley.'

'Come off it,' he snorted. 'Your grandmother is as big a kook as you are. How capture the valley?'

'It's getting too crowded in Ohio,' she told him. 'We Russels need more room for expansion.'

'So?'

'So we adopted the old Irish tradition. If you can't beat them, out-populate them!'

He retaliated by an all-out assault on her foot, tickling her until her giggles woke the baby up. He backed away from the cradle, hands behind his back.

'You can pick him up,' she said, trying to hide the grin. 'He's near unbreakable at three months.' Harry bent over the cradle, slid one huge hand under the baby's shoulders and head, and lifted him out as if he were a crate of eggs. Kate took the little bundle, unfastened her bikini top, and began to nurse the child. Her husband watched, fascinated. 'He's pretty big, but he's lost all his hair?' He tried to make it a statement, but it came out a question.

'Yes, Harry, he's pretty big. As big as his father one of these days. And he's got that little tuft of hair right up in front. Red, without a doubt.' They both watched as the child slurped his fill, and went back to sleep. Kate stretched him out on the lounger, changed his diapers and shirt, and popped him back into the cradle, just as Mary came back out to take her turn at baby-sitting. They transferred the child to the pushchair, still fast asleep, and Mary went off to the orchard with him.

Katie leaned back in the lounger, and stretched. It was a perfect world. Her husband was watching her with those piercing eyes. 'How come you're not down the cellar inventing something?' she queried. 'We have a lot of mouths to feed nowadays.'

'Not to worry,' he returned. 'We're fixed for the next four or five years. Besides, I have to know what people need before I can invent anything to satisfy them!'

'Well, invent something for me,' she teased. 'Invent me a new heaven.'

'Easiest thing in the world,' he laughed, as he swung her up in his arms and started for the house. 'Upstairs, second room on the left, madame. Would you like stars, too?'

She would.

Harlequin ♦ Presents

Coming Next Month

895 STORM Vanessa Grant
After being stranded by a fierce storm in the Queen Charlotte Islands a reporter doubts herself, the hard-hitting pilot she desires and her commitment to a childhood sweetheart.

896 LOSER TAKE ALL Rosemary Hammond
A wealthy American doesn't exactly win his new bride in a poker game. But it amounts to the same thing, because it's marriage for them—win or lose!

897 THE HARD MAN Penny Jordan
Desire for a virtual stranger reminds a young widow and mother she is still a woman capable of love, capable of repeating the mistake she made ten years ago.

898 EXPLOSIVE MEETING Charlotte Lamb
A lab technician's boss resents his employee's impassioned plea on behalf of a brilliant scientist who keeps blowing up the lab. And he misinterprets her persistence—in more ways than one!

899 AN ALL-CONSUMING PASSION Anne Mather
When her father's right-hand man comes to the Caribbean to escort the boss's daughter back to London, she tries to make him forget his responsibilities—never thinking she is playing with fire.

900 LEAVING HOME Leigh Michaels
A young woman never dreams her guardian's decision to remain single had anything to do with her, until he proposes marriage—to pull her out of yet another scrape.

901 SUNSTROKE Elizabeth Oldfield
Can a widow reconcile receiving twenty thousand pounds to pay off her late husband's creditors with leaving the man she loves—even though he's been groomed to marry someone else?

902 DANGEROUS MOONLIGHT Kay Thorpe
It is possible that the Greek hotel owner a vacationer encounters isn't the same man who ruined her sister's marriage. But can she risk asking him outright, when the truth could break her heart?

Available in July wherever paperback books are sold, or through Harlequin Reader Service.

In the U.S.
901 Fuhrmann Blvd.
P.O. Box 1397
Buffalo, N.Y. 14240-1397

In Canada
P.O. Box 2800, Postal Station A
5170 Yonge Street
Willowdale, Ontario M2N 6J3